SILVER'S ASCENT

MEGAN MARIE FRANEY

MEGAN MARIE FRANEY
P.O Box 462, Baldwin, WI 54002
Website: meganmfraney.com

First Edition 2021

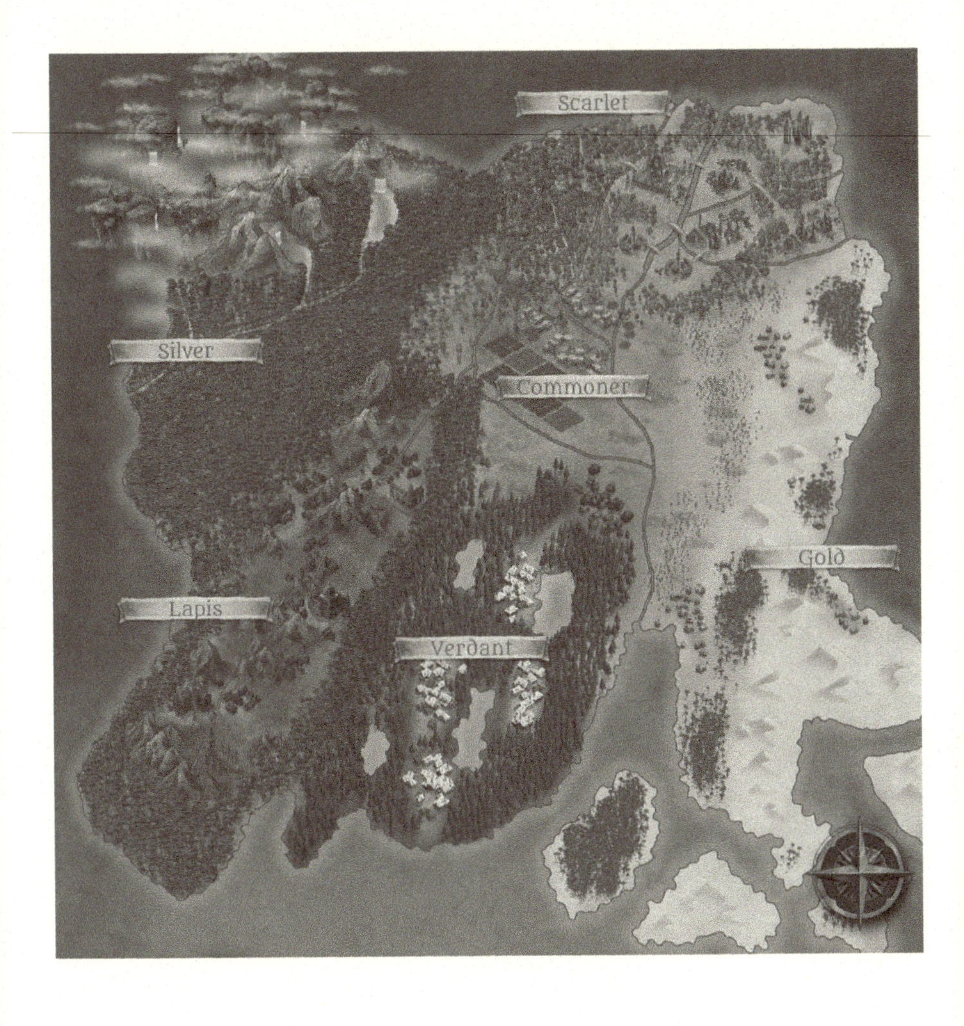
Scarlet
Silver
Commoner
Gold
Lapis
Verdant

PROLOGUE

Moonlight ricocheted off the heavy armor of each Mystic's body as they marched into the dismal Commoner village. The frigid winter air and dirty slush did little to slow their pace. Greed and revenge coursed through their veins as they moved like a hungry shadow, consuming even the tiniest flicker of candlelight.

One Mystic stood out among the rest, broad shoulders, sharp jawline and eyes like jewels. He had all the grace of a lion on the prowl after smelling fresh blood. His heart beat with a fever at the thought of finding the rogue Mystic and making him pay. Tonight was his night to prove himself, he thought. Disgust crinkled his nose as he scanned the dilapidated buildings. It was beyond him how anyone could live in these kinds of cramped and bare conditions.

As they reached the center of the village, they

simultaneously came to a halt. Only the practiced eye would have seen the signal given by the commander. Silence fell over the village as mothers gripped their children and lovers clung to one another in the darkness.

"You know your orders," the commander barely raised his voice. "And kill any that get in your way." A smirk pulled at scarlet lips.

The armor-clad Mystics spread out, kicking in doors, and dragging anyone they could get their hands on out into the freezing winter. Screams echoed through the village as each house was turned upside down.

From a small bedroom window, a pair of violet eyes watched as her village was forced from their dreams and into a nightmare. Terror gripped her as flames danced across her reflection in the dirt-streaked window. Another scream tore through the night and the little girl jumped down from her place in the window and onto her bed.

Running down the hall to her parents, she came up empty. Her heart jumped around in her chest, making her breaths come quick and shallow. She could hear the Mystics banging on the door of her neighbor's house as tears started to prick her eyes. Pure adrenaline propelled her forward as she threw open the door to her older brother's room.

Empty.

The sharp sting of panic shot through her like a lightning bolt. Gooseflesh prickled her skin as she hurtled down the stairs, fearing the worst- that her family was already dead. Tripping on the last step, she flew forward, landing face-first on the cold wood surface, but she was too terrified to feel it.

"Damnit all," her father cursed.

Picking herself back up, she saw her mother and father huddled in the corner of the room, their eyes wild with fear.

"Eli, get her in the closet and stay out of sight," their father ordered.

Just as the door swung closed on the closet, the front door to their house burst open.

"It's going to be okay, Willow," Eli whispered into his sister's ear as he pulled her close. She leaned into his comforting embrace as something was thrown against a wall and shattered on the other side of the door.

"No, please," their mother's muffled voice cried. "We've done nothing wrong," she whimpered.

A deep chuckle raised the hairs on the back of Willow's neck. Darkness started to pull at her as the Mystic's illusion spread through the house.

"You've got the wrong family," their father grunted as he was struggling to free himself.

Eli stiffened behind Willow. As she turned to look at him, she barely caught a glimpse of his contorted face before she was consumed by the illusion. Her heart beat wildly in her chest as her mother's screams filled the air.

"We know he's here," one of the Mystics growled.

"Please don't do this," their mother's voice broke on the last word as she fought back tears.

Willow reached out with both hands, searching for her brother, searching for a way out of the darkness, but came up empty. Terror gripped her, stealing her breath and her whole body prickled as if she'd been ducked into a frozen lake.

A pair of arms wrapped around her, and she tried to scream, but the lump in her throat from holding back tears kept her silent.

"I've got you," Eli's voice reached out like a lifeline and slowly the illusion started to fade away.

Willow looked up at her brother and was surprised to see his brow covered in sweat.

"Eli?" Willow whispered.

"Do you feel that?" One of the Mystics' voices reached them in the closet.

Heavy boots moved down the hall in their direction.

"Eli?" She grabbed his arm and pulled, but he kept his focus on the illusion trying to hold it at bay.

The floor creaked like it always did in front of the stairs, and Willow knew the Mystics were only a few steps from uncovering their hiding place. Her ears started to ring and her breath became ragged as Eli grabbed his head with both hands and doubled over. He was no match for them.

The handle on the door jiggled as Eli fell to his knees.

"I'm so sorry, Willow."

Eli looked up to find that his sister was no longer beside him. Reaching out to where she was a moment ago, his hands fell on her invisible shoulders. "By the Gods," he said under his breath as the door to the closet started to open. He shoved Willow's invisible form into the back of the closet and turned to meet his fate.

"Well, well, what do we have here?" The Mystic with gemstone eyes grabbed Eli by the collar and dragged him into the hall. His eyes skated over the dusty coats and mud-caked boots, and landed on the spot Willow stood, but it was as if he was looking right through her. Her heart stopped and she held her breath, waiting to be dragged out of the closet like her brother.

"It's just the one," the Mystic grumbled as he turned away from the closet unaware that another child, perhaps a more gifted child was only a few inches from his grasp.

Willow clung to the frame of the closet and peeked out with one eye, watching as her brother was dragged down the hall. He held his finger up to his mouth, signaling for her to stay quiet and she nodded as tears began to fall from her eyes.

A bearded man pulled a dagger from his hip and grabbed Eli's arm. Dragging the blade across Eli's skin, bright scarlet blood oozed out.

"That's what I thought. You don't belong here." A sick grin pulled at the corner of the Mystic's mouth. Tossing Eli at his parent's feet, he kicked him in the ribs. Willow swore she could hear her brother's bones crack and she had to fight the rage building inside her.

"Careful now. He is one of us, after all, even if he does reek of Commoner," the Mystic guarding the front door warned.

Eli got to his feet, out of breath and holding his side. "Don't punish them. It was my choice to come here."

"And let me guess, you'll never do it again?" The

Mystic at the front door stalked forward as the others chuckled.

"I promise, I'll never return," Eli closed the gap between him and the Mystic, and Willow felt her heart fall into her stomach. She wasn't ready to say goodbye to her brother. "Just let them go," Eli wheezed.

"I'm afraid I can't take you at your word." With a quick flick of his wrist, the other Mystics jumped into action. The bearded man kicked Eli's legs out from under him, while the other two grabbed their parents and held blades to their necks.

"It's not their fault," Eli yelled.

"And yet they will pay the price."

Eli struggled to free himself as tears glistened in his eyes.

As Willow watched her family be torn apart, tears fell freely from her eyes. *This was all my fault,* she thought. If she hadn't begged her brother to visit in the first place, none of this would be happening. He warned her that it was dangerous, but she had no idea it would lead to this. Despair pulled at her, pushing the fear and rage aside. With her anger subsiding, the illusion that was keeping her invisible slowly faded away.

They turned Eli so he was facing their parents.

"I'll do anything. Please, don't hurt them," Eli said breathlessly.

Laughing, the Mystic holding onto their mother said, "I love when they beg."

"I'll make you a deal." The one who seemed to be in charge smirked.

"Yes, anything," Eli agreed, and the Mystic's smile grew.

"Since you're so great at making decisions, you can choose which one will die and which one will live."

"No," Willow whimpered, stepping out of her hiding spot. They all turned to face her.

"Didn't you check the closet?" One of the men turned to another.

"She must have been hiding in the coats." The Mystic looked the girl up and down with disdain as another marched down the hall and scooped her up.

"She's just an innocent child, don't hurt her," their father pleaded.

"Check her," one of the Mystics ordered.

They pulled the cuff of her shirt to expose her wrist. The brand was still an angry red welt on her skin.

"Commoner," the Mystic noted and dropped her arm.

"Very well." They all turned back to the task at hand. "Who will it be?"

"Save your mother." Their father looked between the two of them. "Willow needs her mother."

"I can't condemn you to death," Eli said through tears.

"You can and you will." Their father's voice was stern and he lifted his chin ever so slightly, giving the Mystic better access to his neck. "Do it!"

"No! STOP!" Willow tried her best to wiggle free from her captor, but it was no use. He was too strong.

"Shut her up."

A dirty, sweaty hand fell over Willow's mouth, stifling her protest.

"So, what'll it be? Dear ol' Mom or Dad?"

One of the Mystics sighed, clearly annoyed at the delay and before Eli could answer, a blade was pulled across their mother's throat.

"He was taking too long." The man shrugged without a care in the world as he let their mother's body slump to the floor.

Willow screamed into the hand that was over her mouth as blood poured from her mother's neck. Her brother let out a string of curses and tried to fight the men pulling him out of the house.

"Leave the girl." The one in charge nodded in Willow's direction and the Mystic dropped her like a sack of potatoes. She crawled across the cold wood surface and into her father's open arm. Pulling her to his chest, he clung to her like a lifeline.

"Never forget your place in the world, Commoners." The Mystic's eyes glazed over the body on the floor before heading out the door.

Her father rocked her back and forth as tears streamed down his face. Willow stared at the slumped body as a single tear fell from her mother's frozen eyes. Willow wanted to cry, to let her grief consume her, but all she could feel was rage. She swore to herself that she would become stronger than all the Mystics, and make them pay for her mother's death.

CHAPTER 1

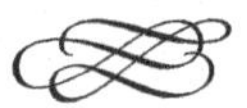

The pink light of dawn stretched across the sparring ring as I finished up my drills. Sweat dripped down my face, and my arms burned. It felt good to get out here and burn off some steam. It might be risky, but it was worth it. Carefully, I went through the steps I had learned so long ago, before my life had changed forever. It was all a game back then. Just something to pass the time with my big brother.

Watch your feet, Wil! I could hear Eli's voice tell me, and I straightened my stance instinctively. Moving the wooden practice sword through the air, I struck at invisible opponents, knocking them down one by one. They all had familiar faces- the Mystics who had killed my mother. Sweat dripped into my eyes as I spun around and shut a pair of gemstone blue eyes forever. I was left panting with exertion, and memory.

When I finished up for the day, I got ready to head

back into town. I stashed the practice sword back in the weapons shed where I had found it, and carefully replaced the lock so that no one could tell I had been there. We weren't allowed real weapons, but these little wooden swords did no harm, and kept the men of the village happy. None of the women were allowed to use the swords, but no one was ever up here this early, so I could train in peace. I learned long ago that the things that made us different were dangerous, and I didn't need anyone to know about my little fighting hobby.

Rising before dawn most days to slip down to the sparring ring, I got in my practice in and was done in time to mingle with the other townsfolk as they headed off to work. Usually, the streets were pretty empty, and slipping through unnoticed was easy. Avoiding other people had become an art that I excelled at most of the time, whether I was invisible or not. The people in the village knew to stay out of my way. Today, things were a little different, and I had to be extra careful.

The Choosing was tomorrow, and in the town center they were erecting a grand stage where the Mystics would stand, towering over the Commoners and reminding us of our place. I rolled my eyes as I watched the men build up the platform. *Mystics,* I thought to myself, shaking my head. Always so dramatic. The townsfolk were excited, because having the Mystics here meant that some of us would be taken away to serve in a Mystic region. Only the lucky got chosen, everyone said. They had no idea what they were in for.

I took a deep breath and slipped into my invisibility

after checking to see that no one was watching me. Once my body was gone, I moved carefully through the crowd, slipping my hands in pockets or bags. It wasn't an honest way to make a living, but I did what I had to for survival. Someone had to feed me and my father.

It had been eleven years since I watched the Mystics murder my mother and steal my brother away from my family. Eleven years of getting by on my own while my father lost himself in the bottom of a bottle, sobering up once in a while for the odd job here and there, and then disappearing right back to his drunkenness. I couldn't bring myself to hate him for it. He had lost his wife and child that night, and every year I crept closer and closer to my twentieth birthday. Closer and closer to being unable to control my abilities, and therefore closer to certain death. I could afford to give the guy a break. Plus, we didn't really need him to do any work. I got enough from my morning walks to hold us over without drawing any attention to us.

All Commoners lived a simple life. We didn't have a choice. We lived in the leftover regions, the pieces of land the Mystics didn't want. My town was one of the lucky ones. Most of us worked in the fields or factories, producing the food that the Mystics ate, so we were able to eat the leftover scraps. They weren't the highest quality, but it was better than some of the other Commoner towns had.

I lost myself in thought for a minute, imagining Eli feasting at a grand table, enjoying food that his father and sister would never get to taste. Eating juicy meat and fresh vegetables that my fellow townsfolk spent their life growing and never using themselves. I imagined what it would be like to bite into soft, freshly baked bread instead of the stale, rock-hard crusts we were given. I wondered if he thought of me and Dad whenever he had a meal, if he knew what things were like for us now.

I was pulled out of my thoughts just in time to avoid crashing into a woman on her way to work. Moving out of the way at the last second, I let my hands dip into her pocket. I felt a few heavy coins, and within moments two of them were being slipped into my own pocket. She would wonder where she misplaced some of her coins, but since I was invisible, she would never know.

The lights in the road started to flicker off as the sun rose higher and they were no longer needed. Sometimes they flickered even before the sun rose, or shut off completely, but at least we had them. They were another perk of living in this village. All the Commoners knew the Mystics had some advanced tech, but they didn't bother sharing it with us. Here, when we would need to rise before the sun, and work past sunset to produce enough to feed them all, they allowed us this small gift. Lights that worked, sometimes, so we could work ourselves to the bone to feed the Mystics.

The walk back to the house was peaceful. We lived a little away from the rest of the village, at the base of a hill beyond the glow of the streetlights. It made us outsiders, but not in a way to draw attention to ourselves. Just the poor father and daughter who had lost their family, and wanted peace, away from nosy neighbors and Mystics looking for trouble. It was the only way to safely hide what I really was.

As I approached my house, I started to get anxious. I had no idea what state I would find my father in. If I was lucky, he would still be asleep, and I could get dressed for school in peace. I had enough to worry about without a confrontation with him. This place was already crawling with Mystics, and it would only get worse tomorrow. I could feel my abilities humming below the surface of my skin, my anxiety lessening the control I had over them. Going invisible today had been a relief, but from now until the Choosing was complete, I couldn't risk it.

The house was silent as I slipped in, and I breathed a sigh of relief. I was too nervous for an argument, and during this time of year Dad usually felt the same. The more Mystics that came to the town, the more irritable we both got. It was best to keep to ourselves. I stripped off my sweaty clothes and jumped into the shower. The water trickled out slowly, and I had to work hard to get myself clean before it became ice cold and I couldn't use it anymore.

I got out of the shower and dried myself off, putting on pants and a loose-fitting top and tied my dark hair up in a bun on the top of my head. I didn't bother trying to look presentable for school. My teachers hated me, and I had too many secrets to make friends with the kids my age. I had grown up a loner, and it was better that way. I only attended because it was required.

I left some coins on the table for my father, hoping he would use them for food and not alcohol, and pocketed the rest for myself. This morning's session in the training field had left me starving, and I needed to keep my strength up to make it through the next couple of days. I would have to steal some bread on my way to class, and hopefully be able to find some meat to buy for lunch. With a quick backwards glance towards my father's room, I stepped out the door and made my way back into town for school.

"Good morning, everyone!" my teacher said with her usual cheeriness. The class was small, just thirty of us. There were other kids my age in the village that had started school with us when we were younger, but most of them had to stop once they hit their teens to help their parents work in the fields or factories. We were the privileged ones, or so everyone said. What it really meant were that we were the ones who got lined up and chosen like cattle for slaughter. At least, that's what it felt like to me. The rest of these kids thought they were getting the opportunity of a lifetime.

As I sat at my table not really paying attention, the rest of the class talked excitedly about which region they'd love to serve in, and what families they wanted to live with. We learned about the noble houses in each region over the course of our schooling, but I never really paid attention. It didn't matter to me whether they were noble or street urchins, there was no such thing as a good Mystic.

CHAPTER 2

I watched the beams of sunlight creep steadily across my room as I lay in bed the next morning. I couldn't sleep last night, not with the Choosing ceremony getting closer and closer. It wasn't that I was in danger of being chosen- only those with top grades who were outstanding members of society were picked to serve the Mystics, neither of which applied to me. The only reason I was even passing my classes was because I convinced my teachers to pass me so they wouldn't have to deal with me creating havoc for another year. I wasn't worried that my name would be called. I just hated this time of year, when my home was crawling with Mystics.

I glanced at my watch and groaned. The ceremony would start in less than half an hour. Normally I'd be okay with waking up before dawn, but I wasn't going to give up sleep for Mystics. Forcing myself out of bed, I slipped into my favorite dirt-stained pants and a loose-fitting top that once belonged to my father. Everyone else would be dressed to impress, so this was my way of mounting a small protest. Let them see what Commoners really looked like every day. I wish I could skip the event entirely, but to do so would court death. Having witnessed the Mystic's punishment up close and personal when they murdered my mother, I knew they didn't make idle threats.

I made my way out of the house and down the path into the main part of the village. The Commoner region was known for old, crummy buildings that could barely hold themselves together, not to mention the garbage littering the streets. Every one of our able-bodied citizens spent their lives growing and preparing food for the Mystics, so the rest of the town responsibilities fell to either the old and infirm, or just didn't get done at all. The only thing that made this village better than the others was the service we performed for the Mystics. It kept us a little better fed that the other Commoner villages, but that was it. We were all kept low by the Mystics so that they could live their privileged lives.

The streets were filled the eligible students and their family members, cheering them on. How anyone could hope for their child, friend, or cousin to be chosen to serve the Mystics was beyond me. We may not have much as Commoners, but I'd rather have nothing and my freedom than serve those murderers.

Keeping my head down, I pushed my way through the crowd, trying to avoid the happy and smiling faces of the ignorant. If there weren't so many Mystics here, I'd risk tapping into my invisibility. But it was much too risky, and my mother hadn't sacrificed everything just for me to out myself because I didn't want to socialize. A round of applause and cheers caught my attention and I cursed under my breath. Ducking and slithering through the crowd, I weaved around a large man only to run smack into someone else.

"Someone's in a rush." The stranger grabbed my shoulders to steady me.

"Yeah well, wouldn't want to be hung for not showing up on time." I shuffled away from him and looked over his shoulder for a path forward.

"I hardly think they'd hang you." I could hear the smile in his voice and turned to look at him.

Curious blue eyes stared into mine and my rebuttal was lost on my tongue. *Not too bad on the eyes there, stranger.* His clothes were clean and pressed in a way that spoke to having buckets of money. Even the most dressed up Commoner didn't look as polished as he did. Which meant he was a Mystic, and had no idea what it was like to be us. As much as I would love to educate him, I didn't have the time or patience.

"I'd rather not find out," I huffed and pushed past him, not bothering to show him any respect.

As I moved through the last of the onlookers I was met by a wall of security. The Mystics always employed Lapis guards to make sure we were all here. If you were caught not attending, they sent their goons to find you and drag you here.

"Willow Knight," I said to the one with a clipboard. He scanned the list and nodded.

"Cutting it close, aren't you?" He motioned for me to join my fellow Choosing candidates.

"Bite me," I said once I was out of earshot. Everyone was lined up in perfect, neat little rows and I joined the last line. It was such a waste of time for me to be here. Everyone knew who the top ten were without the Mystic's lottery system. They could have just collected them from their homes without all this fanfare. This was just a way to show how much control they had over us. We were nothing more than animals to them, meant to be tamed and forced to serve their every need.

Another round of applause rolled through the crowd and a young Mystic walked out onto the stage with a Cheshire cat smile plastered to her face. Judging by her outfit, she was most likely a Scarlet. Scarlets, more than any other Mystic, had a huge flair for the dramatic.

"Welcome to the Choosing, Commoners! I'm sure you're all brimming with excitement to find out who will be chosen this year. But first, I'd like to welcome this year's eligible group! It's so lovely to see so many new and hopeful faces." She wiggled her fingers at someone towards the front like they were long lost friends, and I rolled my eyes. The pageantry of all this was already giving me a headache.

"We come together today," she continued. "To celebrate the children of the Gods. Ten of you will be chosen to serve in one of the four regions: the Golds, the Verdants, the Lapis, and the Scarlets. But let us not forget our fallen brethren, the Silvers. Though there are none left alive, we must still honor their legacy with a moment of silence."

I shifted back and forth, kicking at the tiny rocks in the dirt. We were taught in school that the Silvers went extinct after a war that took place hundreds of years ago, leaving their entire region destroyed, dragons and other mythical creatures left to roam freely. It was against the law to go into the Silver region. There are some who believed the Silvers were still alive. My mother was one of them. She believed that Mystics from the other regions had banded together, led by leaders who despised the Silvers and their power. The story goes that they attacked the Silvers, but their allies had warned them that the attack was coming, and many Silvers escaped and learned how to fit into the other regions without being noticed.

"Before we start choosing the lucky recruits, our representatives from each region will do a demonstration to show you all what your new life could be like if you join us! In a few moments, you'll get to see wonders beyond your imagination! Don't worry, everything you see is just for show! Bring the young children up front so they can get a better view!"

Could you injure yourself simply by rolling your eyes too much? Like sheep, parents started herding their children to the front for the show. It was the same thing every year, idiots crowding around to 'oooh' and 'ahhh' at this ridiculous display of power.

"First up, the Lapis!"

A young man stepped up to the stage dressed in a

tailored dress shirt of light blue, fitted snugly across his chest and tucked into navy blue pants that probably cost more than the entire village's wardrobe combined. Four men followed, carrying up a large log. We kept it in the weapons shed during the year, and the young men rolled it around as a strength exercise during training classes.

With a loud *thunk*, the men dropped the log, some sighing with relief. The Lapis man stepped up to the log with a smirk and stretched his arms and legs, obviously putting on a show for our benefit. We all knew that Lapis were blessed with incredible strength, among other abilities. All but the youngest in the crowd knew what was about to happen. The Lapis bent down and picked up the log like it weighed as little as a feather. He moved it up and down, swung it around the air like a bat, and tossed it a few times. When he let it fall to the stage, I could feel ground shake beneath my feet. It had taken four grown Commoners to bring that log to the stage, but the Lapis had handled it as though it weighed nothing.

The crowd went wild, screaming in disbelief at the unnerving show of strength. As for me, I stayed quiet, thinking about what happened every year when the Choosing was over and the Mystics went home. Although he could have carried it back to the weapons shed easily, the Lapis would leave it on the stage, forcing our men to struggle all the way back up the hill with the heavy log. *Jerks.*

Next, a young woman dressed in a gorgeous, flowing red dress with curling blond hair stepped onto the stage, and I gritted my teeth. I hated all Mystics, but especially the Scarlets. They were the ones who had taken my brother away. They were the ones who killed my mother. Their abilities always unnerved me, and I had to focus on my breathing exercises to stay calm and endure what was to come.

The Scarlets were masters of illusion. As the crowd watched, buzzing in excitement, the young Scarlet smiled warmly and lifted her hands. Suddenly, a loud screech rang out overhead, and a glittering red dragon swooped down on our heads. A lot of the kids screamed and grabbed onto their parents, but the adults knew it was all fake. An illusion meant to inspire and awe us. The illusion was so real that as the dragon drew close I could feel the wind blow across my face as it flapped it's wings, and heat warmed my face as he spewed out his fiery breath. The only time we had ever seen a dragon was during these displays. The Scarlets liked to choose illusions that filled us all with wonder so we could worship at their feet. Everyone knew dragons didn't come this far south. They had been left to roam wild in the Silver mountains after the rest of the regions killed all the Silvers. Or so we were told. Maybe they all had dragons as pets in the Scarlet region. Who knows? I would certainly never find out.

Once everyone had settled down from the Scarlet's display, she left the stage and was replaced by a middle-aged woman in grey pants and an emerald green blouse. This was the demonstration that always infuriated me. Because Verdants had an affinity for nature and animals, they could coax plants back to life, or tell sheep to not stray so far from their flock. Every year, a patch of our field was left to dry out and wither so that a Verdant could come and bring it back to its full glory. Rumor was that the food from that part of the field tasted amazing, but we never got any of it. And why were we working ourselves to the bone, dying in the fields under the hot sun for scraps if the Verdants could come and with a flick of their fingers make it all ripe and beautiful? A load of crap, if you asked me. I didn't even glance over at the newly-grown stalks at the side of the stage. It made me too angry.

If anyone asked me, which they didn't, I would tell them that the only good part of this annoying display was the Gold demonstration. The Golds could read auras, were kind-hearted by nature, and could heal. They were the only group of Mystics that I could tolerate. I craned my neck to see who was approaching the stage. Every year, the Golds chose a sick Commoner from the town to heal. This year, a boy of about twelve was brought onto the stage, carried by his father. A few weeks ago, there had been a terrible accident, and he had fallen from a cart awkwardly and broken his neck. He hadn't been able to walk since. With his eyes streaming with tears and thank you's coming from his lips in a nonstop stream, the father placed his son gently in the seat that had been placed next to where the Gold was standing. Dressed regally in a black suit and deep golden tie, the older Gold Mystic looked down on the child with a smile, and placed his hands upon his head. For a few minutes, nothing happened, but no matter how much time had passed, not a sound was heard from the crowd.

After a few more minutes, the Gold man took his hands away from the boy's head, and held them out, with an encouraging smile. The boy timidly placed his hands in the Gold's and stood up. He moved from foot to foot, twisting his hips and stretching like he had just gotten out of bed after a very good nap. He had been healed. The crowd exploded in cheers, and the boy and his father cried in each other's arms.

Like the Verdant's powers, the Golds had the capability of helping us so much. They could heal sickness, mend broken bones. But instead they hid in their region, only healing those they deemed worthy. Once a year, someone from my village was healed, and it was a miracle, really. The Golds could have chosen to just go up there and read someone's aura, but they didn't. They came a few days before the ceremony and met with the townsfolk that needed healing, choosing whoever was in most need of their help. Some of the kinder ones even healed a few extra people before or after the ceremony. While it was disappointing to be passed over, you could always hope for next year, if you were still around. Most Mystics lived long lives because of their access to the Gold's healing services, but we Commoners had much shorter lifespans. It was unfair, but that's what life as a Commoner was. Unfair.

CHAPTER 3

When the applause died down, the young Mystic who was conducting the ceremony came back on stage, and the Choosing ceremony began.

"Now, let's get to the part you all have been waiting for! Once your name is called, you'll have the opportunity to say a few words to the crowd, and then it's off to say goodbye to your family and hello to your new life."

She paused, and of course the idiots around me all cheered at the thought of being ripped from their family to be a slave for the rest of their days.

"Without further ado, let's announce who the first Chosen is," she looked down at the device in her hands and back up at the crowd. "Finnley Woods, you've been chosen to serve the Verdants!"

The crowd erupted with applause and Finnley ran up to the stage, waving and smiling like a buffoon.

The Mystic moved aside for him to address us. "I just

want to say that I'm so grateful to be Chosen and I hope I've made my family proud." A few cheers rang out behind me, clearly Finnley's family rooting him on. He waved once more and made his way off the stage with a guard close behind him. He was theirs now, and until he was safely on the ship the Mystics weren't going to let him out of their sight.

Looking at my watch, I tuned out the rest of the ceremony. Another name was called, another speech was given, another round of applause. It was all the same and it took every shred of control I had to not let my abilities take over and disappear.

"Alright, we have one name left this year. Who's it going to be?" The Mystic cooed with excitement.

I turned to leave, knowing my name wouldn't be called and there was no reason for me to listen to another speech.

"Willow Knight." I froze mid-step and felt like someone had dumped a bucket of ice water over my head. I wasn't the only one in shock. Everyone around me gasped and turned to stare. For a moment I thought it must be a mistake. There was no chance I'd be picked, and everyone knew it.

"Don't be shy, come on up, Willow." The Mystic encouraged. "You've been Chosen to serve the Scarlets!" her voice repeated, clearly annoyed and disappointed in me for not running up to the stage the moment my name was called.

This can't be happening, I thought.

My legs started to move on their own accord as my

brain tried to wrap itself around the notion that I was Chosen. The crowd was silent as I made my way toward the podium. There was no applause for me and hatred dripped off of everyone I passed. I had obviously taken someone's spot.

"Cheater," someone said under their breath. "Bitch," someone else snickered. "Ungrateful bastard."

As I reached the stage, I was rushed up the stairs and in front of the crowd.

"What wise words do you have to share with everyone?" The Mystic grinned, trying to give me another chance to show my excitement and appreciation.

At first, I didn't respond. I didn't want to serve anyone at all, especially people who thought they were better than everyone else because they'd been born with a *skill* or two. She handed me the microphone, and I took it as my hands shook. "I am going to do my best to improve our society," the words left my mouth before I could think. "And to serve," I added quietly, but it sounded unconvincing.

Wait. Why was I droning on like the rest of these idiots? They couldn't take back who was Chosen, it was too late. This was my last moment of freedom. I'd rather speak the truth.

"Actually, screw this. I didn't want to be Chosen. I hate the Mystics! I won't serve them well. I'll make sure they get what is coming to them, if it's the last thing I do!" I dropped the mic. The loud screech of the microphone followed, leaving everyone covering their ears. I shrugged with a smile.

The Scarlet's eyes locked onto mine for a moment

before she motioned for me to leave. If looks could kill, I would have never made it off the stage.

I jogged off the stage and closed my eyes, feeling the warm breeze whip through my hair and taking deep breaths. I still couldn't believe I'd been Chosen. *Me*. I was beyond perplexed as to why they'd want me when I'd excelled at absolutely nothing that made me a good candidate to serve. My speech just now was all the proof they needed that they had made a mistake.

At least I'd get the opportunity to make a Mystic's life miserable, I thought, and I couldn't help but smile.

I pushed my way through the crowd, wanting to get home quickly and see my father one last time before they shipped me off to the Scarlets. Taking a shortcut, I ditched my security detail and cut through an alley that opened up into a field.

Running as fast as I could through the thick brush, I tripped over a rock and tumbled into the dirt. A sharp, stinging sensation ached across my palm.

Shoot.

I picked myself back up, turned my hand over, and looked at my palm. Bright silver blood dripped onto the brown grass. Fear prickled through me as my blood glistened in the bright morning sun. I looked around, panicked. If anyone saw what I really was, being shipped off to serve the Scarlets would be the least of my worries. Quickly, I turned my shirt inside out and wiped the blood off my hand. Kicking at the dirt, I covered the spot where a few drops of silvers were still visible. I pressed my hands together to try and stop the bleeding as I made my way home more carefully.

I could hear voices in the distance. They were coming for me already.

I burst through the front door. "Dad?"

"Willow?" His eyes met mine and my heart felt like it was going to fall out of my chest.

"You were Chosen, weren't you?"

All I could do was nod.

"You're sober," I exhaled in shock. I took a closer look at him. His blonde hair was now mostly grey and lifeless and his ivory skin had given way to a sickly complexion from all the drink. He was a far cry from the man he once was, but who could blame him?

I moved toward the kitchen slowly as if he was a small woodland creature who might spook at any second.

"It's not all bad." He ignored my observation. "This could be the start of a brand new life for you." He pulled me in for a hug, his arms crushing me against him. My stomach hollowed at his words, and my heart ached.

I pulled away and looked up into his dark, ink-colored eyes. "I don't want a new life. I don't know why they picked me."

He gave me a tight-lipped smile that reminded me of Eli. The two were spitting images of each other, while I looked more like my mother with each passing day. "You're worth far more than you give yourself credit for."

His flattery was unexpected. Really, everything about this morning was unexpected. I was still reeling from the fact that he was sober and completely aware of his surroundings.

"Still, I'd rather stay here with you and keep what's left of our family together." I tried to keep my voice calm and even, but he still winced at my words.

"That's the thing about family, Willow. No matter the distance, we will always be together. Even your mother hasn't left your side. I see her in you every day." He reached out and touched my cheek.

I let his words sink in. We hardly ever talk about Mom, or Eli for that matter. It was too hard for him to acknowledge everything we lost, and it always ended with him at the bottom of a bottle.

"I miss her." I couldn't look at him for fear that this moment might crumble right before my eyes.

"I miss her, too," he sighed and gave me another hug. "Alright, off with you. You don't want to be late."

I let out a heavy breath. The thought of leaving him now, when he needed me the most, was something that my head couldn't wrap itself around. He was *sober*. I could barely comprehend it. He was improving for the first time in years – and now I had to leave? What kind of crap was that?

The sound of boots coming up the path caught my attention. *I should have more time,* I thought. I couldn't help but regret the words I spoke at the ceremony. There was no question they were the reason the Mystic guards weren't giving me more time with my dad. They wanted to punish me.

There was a knock at the door and my heart started to

pound immediately. Memories of the night my mother had died always rushed back when I heard a knock like that. I could feel my abilities kick into over-drive. I wanted to disappear, but deep down I knew that would only lead to my father being punished for my disappearance.

"I don't want to go."

"You're going to do great." He cupped my cheek. "I am so proud of the young woman you've become. Stay true to who you are and never forget where you came from."

"I won't." Tears stung my eyes, but I refused to let them spill over.

He opened the door and three large men pushed their way into the house.

"Willow Knight?"

"Here," I sighed and stepped forward, letting them guide me out of the house.

As I started down the path, I looked over my shoulder at our little cottage on the hill. Streams of sunlight crisscrossed through the large oak tree's branches, blanketing the cottage with beautiful morning light. For the first time in a long time, I didn't see the patched board-and-batten sides or the lopsided rocky roof. Nor did I see the shabby, weather-worn wood that looked barnacled and sun-bleached. Instead, I saw a home, *my* home, and the family that I'd lost forever.

CHAPTER 4

My body jostled back and forth as if the Gods themselves were trying to force us from the sky. And who could blame them? People were not meant to fly- the fact that my stomach now resided somewhere in my chest was proof of that. A mechanical whirring and sharp jolt sent a pang of fear through me, and I had to fight my instincts as they bubbled to the surface. Now was so not the time for my abilities to take over.

There was a loud bang, and my whole body vibrated. This was it. We were all going to die, and I was never going to get the chance to ruin a Mystic's day. One of the guards who had dragged me from my home and strapped me into this death bird moved in front of me and unbuckled my harness.

"What are you doing?" I grabbed onto each side of my seat.

"This is your stop." He grabbed me by the arm and ripped me out of my seat. "Time to get off," he yelled over the roar of the engine.

He placed his hand up to a screen on the wall and a piece of the ship slid away. Adrenaline pumped through my veins as the late afternoon sun blinded me. The guard pushed me forward and I stumbled to the top of the stairs leading to the ground just a few feet below me.

"Oh, thank the Gods," I said under my breath when I realized we were no longer in the air.

As I reached the bottom step, I looked back at the ship that had delivered me to my prison. The exterior was smooth and sleek, shining brightly in the sun. Never in all my years had I seen anything like it.

"Willow Knight?" A woman called my name, pulling me back to reality. I jumped off the last step and moved toward her. "Welcome to the Scarlet Region." A big smile was plastered to her perfectly made-up face. She looked to be about my age, but the way she carried herself seemed much older.

A loud buzzing pulled my attention back to the ship as it began to disappear. I could still hear the power coming from the engine, but within a few seconds the sound was gone, and it was as if it was never there to begin with.

"Come along." The woman grabbed my arm and started to pull forward. She was nicer about it than the guard, but being yanked around like a doll was starting to get on my nerves.

"Are you…I mean…am I serving you?" I caught up and stepped in line with her.

"No," she dropped my arm. "I'm here to escort you to your new home with the Starr family."

"So, what, are they too busy to come get me themselves?" I snorted.

She stopped in her tracks. "Yes, they are. And I suggest you get your attitude under wraps before it gets you in far more trouble than you could ever dream of."

I rolled my eyes. "Believe me, I'm well aware of how horrible Mystics can be."

Her lips formed a hard line and her nostrils flared. She looked like she wanted to knock me into next week, but thought better of it.

"Just follow me," she said.

As we left the landing area, I was captivated by the different sounds and smells of this new place. There was a sweetness to the air that I couldn't quite put my finger on, and a soft melody reached my ears as a group of people my age passed us laughing and joking.

Must be nice not to have a care in the world.

"You'll be serving the Starr brothers," my escort said, pulling me from my reverie. "They are the most powerful Scarlets, perhaps even Mystics, anyone has seen in generations. Their family rules this region."

"Then why would they pick me?" I said under my breath.

"It's a mystery, really." She looked me up and down, wrinkled her nose, and motioned for me to keep up.

Turning away from the hustle and bustle, she led me toward an arcade structure that was bigger than anything we had back home. White bricks were stacked into perfect arches that towered above me, and as we passed under the first arch I looked up and noticed that the legs of the pillars shot up from the ground to form a giant 'X' above my head. I'd never seen anything so intricate that was purely for decoration in my entire life.

Vines grew up the pillars with tiny white flowers that had a soft aromatic fragrance, giving the air that sweet smell I couldn't identify earlier.

"Aaron is the eldest son of the Starr household," the woman blathered on. "He runs the day-to- day now that his parents are spending more time away from the region. While his father is still the leader, Aaron has taken up most of his responsibilities, and we expect Mr. Starr to pass the title down to his son shortly. And of course, there's Jayce. He's..." She paused and bit her lip. "Well, let's just say the apple fell far from the tree with him."

"That's reassuring," I grumbled. I really didn't want to find out what she meant.

Her ebony eyes pierced through me, and she frowned. "You should be grateful you were chosen to serve the Starrs."

"Right," I drawled out, rolling my eyes. "Grateful. That's me." I smirked.

She spun on me, and I almost walked right into her. "You are one of the God's weakest creations. I suggest you learn to bite that tongue of yours, or we can find a creative way to remove it from your mouth."

"If you don't think I'm fit for the job, I'd be happy to go back and send someone else in my place."

"How dare you," she practically snarled.

A loud screeching pierced my eardrums. Squeezing my eyes shut, I put my hands over my ears and dropped to the ground. The pain was all-consuming, and I collapsed onto the warm stone. I tried to call on my abilities to block out the pain, but there was nothing but emptiness.

The ringing stopped and I was able to breathe again as the pain subsided. "What did you do to me?" I panted as anger bubbled through my blood. As I pushed to my feet, I noticed a few people had gathered to see what was going on. I'm sure they couldn't wait to see pain inflicted on a Commoner.

"That was a warning." She waved her hand at the crowd, and they started to disperse. "And it doesn't even come close to what the Starr brothers will do to you if you don't get that smart mouth of yours in order," she smirked, clearly proud of herself.

"Shweed," I whispered as we continued down the path.

As the word fell off my lips, a pit in my stomach grew. It was a word my mom used all the time, a cross between a shit head and a weed. My dad used to make fun of her all the time for it.

We spent the rest of the walk in silence, and that was fine with me. If she thought her little parlor trick was meant to scare me into submission, she was dead wrong. All it did was prove that Mystics had no regard for Commoners, and one day I'd make sure she'd pay for her little 'lesson'.

We walked up the winding stone path, and I was out of breath by the time we reached the top. Finally reaching our destination, she entered a code into a screen and the gate slowly swung open.

"Oh my Gods," my mouth fell open. "This is a house for two people?"

It was six stories tall with floor to ceiling windows on the upper floors. The tan stone exterior was lit up by the setting sun and a turquoise pool covered the area to my right. I didn't even know water could be that blue, and I couldn't help but wonder if it was unnatural.

The front door was at least three times my five foot five inches, and as it swung open, a woman with a huge smile plastered on her face and dark, pixel like eyes blinked at the sight of me.

"Welcome to the Starr residence, may I inquire as to who you are?"

"Is she, are you-" I looked between my escort and the woman-type thing in the doorway.

"Yes, I am an artificial intelligence unit named Alice." Her head cocked to the side and her pixel eyes blinked.

A thrum of excitement bubbled in my chest and a part of me hated that anything about this place was enticing in any way. But an AI? We grew up hearing fantastic stories about the kind of technology that existed in the Mystic regions, and it always sounded too good to be true.

"Alice, this is Willow Knight, the new Commoner here to serve." The woman spoke clear and loud as if Alice was deaf. "I'll leave her in your charge. Please give my best to the Starrs."

"Ah, yes, we've been expecting you." She motioned me

into the house with a gentle hand guiding me. Leave it to the non-human to treat me with some dignity.

I couldn't believe this was my new home. Just thinking the word *home* sent a shiver down my spine. *No.* This wasn't my new home; this was just where I was living...for now. But I had to admit, living here would be a lot easier to get used to than I originally thought.

"Right this way, Willow." She started down a long hallway, and I followed her, looking around.

Chandeliers hung on the ceiling far above my head, making them look tiny in comparison to the rest of the house. Family portraits hung proudly for all to see, and my heart ached at the sight. I couldn't help but feel jealous that the Starrs not only had the picture-perfect family but that they had pictures at all. My mother and Eli lived only in my memory, and the edges had started to fade.

"What do you know of the Starr family?"

"Err, nothing really." For the first time since I landed, I felt self-conscious. Between Alice and this house, it was so very clear that I didn't belong.

"They are one of the most powerful families of the Scarlet Region. They hold a great influence over many of the laws and regulations that have been put in place over the years across all regions. Aaron Starr took over the day-to-day operation a few years ago with his brother, Jayce Starr, as his right-hand man. He'll inherit the leadership fully sometime very soon."

"The woman who brought me here made it seem like Jayce was different, or there was something off about him?" I inquired. I wondered how much her programming would allow me to ask.

"He is very powerful, and a true-blooded Scarlet. His abilities are at their fullest potential, but he does like to keep to himself. There are some who would speak ill of Jayce and Aaron. Whether it comes from jealousy or just run of the mill gossip, I assure you, it's not worth your time." She gave me another perfect smile.

Apparently, there was a limit to what she could say. I'd have to test that line while I was here and see if I could find a way around her programming.

She led to a metal portion of the wall and stopped in front of it. Two doors slid open, and another small room appeared on the other side. She stepped inside and motioned for me to follow.

"Come along, you don't want to keep them waiting."

I shook my head as my fight or flight instinct kicked in. My abilities bubbled to the surface and my vision started to blur at the corner of my eyes.

"What is this?" I asked, trying to keep my abilities from taking over.

Alice giggled, "An elevator. Almost all the buildings in this region have them. The Scarlets chose to build up rather than wide to preserve the habitat. It allows us to get from one floor to another quickly and efficiently."

"I'd rather take the stairs." I looked from side to side.

"Don't be silly, you don't want to be sweating and out of breath for your first meeting with the Starr brothers."

"A little sweat never hurt anyone."

Alice stepped forward and gripped my arm. "You have

nothing to be afraid of." Her fingers wrapped around my wrist, and even though I already knew she wasn't human, the way she gripped me made it clear. There was no amount of fighting that would loosen the steel-tight hold she had on me.

Taking a hesitant step forward, I entered the small space. The doors slid shut behind me and she let go of my wrist. Pressing a button with the number six on the panel in front of her, the whole room jolted upward.

My stomach felt like it was going to fall out of my body. What was with the Mystic's obsession with being launched into the sky?

There was a loud ding, and we came to a halt. The doors slid open once more and Alice stepped out of the contraption and into a room that was larger than ten of my kitchen's back home.

Floor to ceiling windows made up the walls, and an orange glow filled the room as the sun set outside.

"Mr. Aaron, Mr. Jayce, the new recruit is here to meet you."

I hadn't even noticed the two brothers sitting on a sofa off to one corner. I was too distracted by the fact that I could see almost the whole region from up here.

"Thank you, Alice." A deep, familiar voice pulled my attention away from the windows.

Blue eyes caught mine and the corner of his lips twitched. All of the blood drained from my face and my heart felt like it jumped into my throat. "It's you."

CHAPTER 5

The stranger's eyes held mine and he cocked his head to the side as if he'd already forgotten me. "You were at the Choosing," I tried to remind him. "I ran into you and-"

"Please tell me you weren't mingling with Commoners again?" The other brother, a tall blonde with a nasty look on his face, cut me off as they both stepped toward me.

"Just keeping an eye on our investments," he said to his brother, never taking his eyes off of me. There was something about his gaze that made me feel exposed and anxious, like he could see the color of my blood just by looking at me.

"Let's hope that's all you were doing." His steely gaze made the hairs on the back of my neck stand up. "I'm in no mood to clean up any more of your messes at the moment."

The blonde brother who I hadn't met at the Choosing

ceremony turned to me and said, "Since you're already well acquainted with my brother, Jayce," his eyes flicked between the two of us as he stepped forward. "Allow me to introduce myself, I'm Aaron, head of this household." Looking me up and down, he wrinkled his nose like I was a stain on his perfectly clean floors. My abilities hummed inside me as his eyes slowly made it to my face once again. "And while you'll serve both of us, you'll get your orders from me."

I glanced at Jayce, and back at his brother. There was an odd tension between them I didn't understand. They were brothers, after all, and they got to live together every day. How could they be anything but happy?

"You'll find a list in your quarters of what's expected of you. Starting with a bath and a change of clothes." He took a step back. "Commoner or not, we can't have you looking like you rolled out of the swamp while you serve under this household."

"There's nothing wrong with my clothes," I spat back. They might not be much, but they were all I had left of home.

"Rule number one," he said through gritted teeth. "Don't speak unless you're asked to."

I opened my mouth to tell him where he could shove it, but out of the corner of my eye, Jayce shook his head ever so slightly.

With the taste of my retort still on my tongue, Aaron continued. "Should you fail to complete anything on your list you will receive punishment. And though you are new here, there will be no leniency for tardy work."

My heart pounded in my chest and some of the bravado I'd felt just a moment ago started to disappear. Aaron's eyes were murderous, and I knew without a doubt he'd hurt me and he'd enjoy it, just like the Mystic who killed my mother.

"Should you have any questions about your assignments, Alice is here to help you. Don't come to me. Understood?" He cocked his head to the side and stared at me.

"Oh, can I talk now?" I blurted.

Aaron looked to his brother and back to me with a wicked grin.

A dozen Mystics ran into the room, swords drawn, yelling for me to get on my knees. Aaron and Jayce had completely disappeared as one of the Mystics kicked me in the back and forced me to the ground. I barely caught myself when something heavy pressed into the middle of my back and forced my face down on the cold tile floor. My abilities pressed at every corner of my mind as terror shot through me like a lightning bolt.

"Take her hands first," one of the Mystic's growled.

"What? No! Please."

The blade came down in one swing and pain shot up my arm and through my body.

I heard my scream from outside of myself and I could feel everything and nothing all at once as my abilities pressed against the thick layer of fear surrounding me. Then it hit me. *This was an illusion.* The moment I realized it, the effect started to fade, and the Mystics who were holding me down vanished into thin air. Holding my hands out in front of me, I sighed with relief. They were still very much attached to my arms.

Tearing my gaze from my hands, I looked up at the Starr brothers once more. Aaron's eyes bore into mine and his lips formed a hard line.

Shoot, I really did it this time, I thought. Did he feel my abilities pushing against his? Is that why he dropped the illusion? I knew better than to fight against their little tricks, but I wasn't expecting him to attack me out of nowhere like that. I took a deep, shaky breath as the effects of the illusion and the swell of my abilities wore off. I was going to have to keep my guard up now that I was living with Mystics.

"Are you just going to stare at her all day, or can we be done with this?" Jayce asked.

"One last thing," Aaron looked me up and down. "Should you disobey or step out of line, your father will be the one to pay the price." He eyes bore into mine. "So be a good little girl, for your dad's sake."

Aaron looked me up and down once more and then turned to his brother. "I'm finished," he turned his back, clearly dismissing me. "For now."

Jayce looked at his brother and then back at me. "I have high hopes for you and your ability to serve." He folded his arm over his chest. "No matter what you said at the Choosing ceremony, I think you'll find yourself quite happy here."

"Not likely," I said under my breath.

"Alice?" Jayce said, looking away from me. If he heard me, for some reason he was choosing to ignore it. "Please take Willow to her room and acquaint her with the rest of the house. We wouldn't want her slipping up on her first day, now, would we?"

"Of course, Mr. Jayce. Is there anything else I can do for you now?" Alice's chipper voice came from behind me.

"That'll be all." Jayce nodded his head once and rejoined his brother without so much as a glance in my direction.

Alice placed her hand on the small of my back and guided me toward the metal box. The moment the doors slid open, I stepped inside without hesitation. Though I was still wary of the moving death-box, I was also desperate to be out of the brother's presence. Aaron was a certified jerk, and Jayce, while he wasn't outright hostile, clearly had some sort of angle going on.

Alice pressed the button with the number two on it and the ground fell out from under me. Or at least, that's what it felt like. I really needed to find the stairs in this place.

I jumped as another ding sounded from the metal contraption, and the doors opened in response. I was back on solid ground once more.

"You'll find the kitchen on this floor." She walked off the elevator and I quickly followed behind her. She pointed out the main dining hall with a table that had enough seating for me, my father, and all our neighbors back home, as well as the kitchens. I was quickly introduced to another Commoner named Jack, who was pulling fresh loaves of bread from the oven when we arrived in the kitchen. The smell of wheat and herbs made my mouth water, and my stomach groaned with hunger.

"Nice to meet you, Willow! Welcome to the Starr household. I'm sure you'll be very happy here!"

I doubt that.

"Hi Jack. How long have you been serving the Starrs?" He looked a little older than I was, but didn't come from my village.

"I was Chosen 8 years ago."

"And do you always work in the kitchens?"

"Oh, no! Anne, the cook, asked me to help her out since she was busy with dinner when the breads were done. I help her in here sometimes, but I mostly just do anything the Starr brothers ask of me. No two days are the same!"

Great.

He put together a quick basket of leftovers for me and sent us on our way. Today had been such a whirlwind I couldn't even remember if I had eaten anything before leaving the house this morning, and I was grateful that they were at least feeding me.

I followed Alice through the rest of the house, picking at a slice of bread as she pointed out various rooms and locations that I assumed would fall to me to take care of. The bread was soft. Really soft. So soft I didn't even have to chew it. *Ugh, did they have to make this so difficult to hate?* Once the tour was finished, we made our way back to the death-box. I groaned.

"Aren't there any stairs in this place?" I said, more to myself than to Alice.

"Yes, of course, but no one uses them. They aren't very efficient."

"Can you show me?" I asked as I shoved another bite of bread into my mouth.

Moving away from the elevator, she turned back the way we had come and walked to the end of the hall. She pulled on a latch that I hadn't noticed before and a door swung open toward us.

"Does it go all the way to the top floor?" I asked peeking my head into the stairwell and looking upward.

"You can reach every floor from this staircase except the penthouse." Her pixel eyes blinked at me and though her expression was neutral, I felt like she was judging me for some reason.

"Lead the way to my room." I pointed toward the stairs.

Alice gave me a small smile and started up the staircase. Once we'd climbed to the third floor, she grabbed hold of another latch and pushed the door open. I was going to have to start paying more attention to the little things in this place. Everything was hidden and tucked out of sight.

Following Alice down a short hallway, I notice there were only a few doors in this corridor.

"Welcome to your new home!" She motioned toward a door on the left.

"Who do the other rooms belong to?" I looked down the hall at the other closed doors.

"To the other Commoners who serve here."

"How many others are here?"

"Well, you met Jack. There are five others- Joseph, Kerry, Paula, Michael, and Jaqueline. Each one lives on this floor, along with the cook, Anne, who is actually a Verdant, so she lives in town."

As Alice was speaking, a head popped out from one of the doors.

"Hi there!" A middle-aged woman stepped into the hallway. "I'm Paula. Welcome to the Starr house!"

Ugh, was everyone going to be so enthusiastic about this?

"Nice to meet you," I answered, trying to be polite.

Something *pinged* at her side, and she picked up a small tablet.

"I've got to go. I hope you get settled in ok! If you need anything, just knock on my door, dear."

She rushed down the hallway and into the elevator.

"I will let you get acquainted with where you'll be staying," Alice said when Paula had left. "Fresh clothes have been left for you and there's a bathroom inside your quarters where you can get cleaned up." She pushed the door open and motioned inside. "Your bag was delivered while you were speaking with Mr. Aaron and Mr. Jayce." She pointed to the foot of my bed.

"My bag?" I said under my breath. It was mandatory for anyone who went to the Choosing to pack their bag in case they got Chosen, but I never bothered to pack one. My father must have done it for me, and the thought brought tears to my eyes.

"I do hope you enjoy your time here and if you need

anything, just call out my name." Before I could respond, she disappeared.

I quickly closed the door behind me and made my way into the room. It looked like it was built for the Gods.

The charcoal-colored walls didn't give the room a cold, dark feeling like I would have expected. Instead, the whole room felt warm and inviting. White linen curtains hung effortlessly on each side of the window, and I'd never seen fabric so crisp and devoid of dust.

I strolled over to the couch across the room and ran my fingers over the intricate pattern. The warm cream fabric was embroidered with leaves in fine green silk that looked so delicate, I could swear they'd sprouted with the spring and sunk into the couch. The number of hours it must have taken to sew each one for a couch almost no one would see seemed like a complete waste of time.

I stretched out across the sofa and the cushions wrapped around my body like a hug. The large window on the wall was enormous, letting the soft twilight light fill the room as one or two stars started to become visible.

Looking up at the sky made me think of my brother. I was closer than I had ever been to Eli. Maybe now that we were both living in the Scarlet region, we could be a family again. I wondered if he knew that I was Chosen or if he kept tabs on us from afar. The thought made my heart race and renewed the small hope I had left of bringing our family back together. Dad might not be with us just yet, but with Eli and I working together, maybe we could find a way to make our family whole again.

Thinking about my dad reminded me of the bag he'd

packed. Sitting up and making my way to the foot of the bed, I unzipped the duffel.

My favorite knit sweater with a hole in the sleeve sat on top. I pulled it up to my nose and took a deep breath. It smelled like grass, spices, and musky wood. Like home. My heart swelled as I imagined my father going about the house and packing a little slice of home for me to keep with me.

There were a few more items of clothing and a book of short stories that he used to read to me when I was a kid, but that's not what caught my attention.

At the bottom of the bag, tucked off to one side was an envelope with my name on the front written with a shaky hand. It felt too heavy to just be a note and so I ripped it open and carefully dumped the contents on the bed. There was a small, folded piece of paper with one short sentence written across the middle of the page, '*used to be your moms*', along with a silver necklace.

I picked up the beautiful piece of jewelry and turned it over on my palm. *Kayja* was inscribed on the back, my mother's name, and on the front was the beautiful triquetra symbol for family, unity, and protection. My mom wore this necklace every day of her life. As I pulled up an image of her in my head, I held the necklace to my chest and took a deep breath.

I picked up the book of short stories and crawled into bed to read up on the people I was now going to be surrounded by. "Stupid Mystics," I grumbled as I skipped the first few stories and flipped to a page titled "God of the Winds".

Adais, God of the Winds, and Niulla, Goddess of the Elements, had three children: Kayja, Irus, and Lethos."

I smiled at the name Kayja and touched the necklace around my neck.

The firstborn, Irus, was favored by both of his parents. He became God of Knowledge, and had a keen sense of nature. He created the first generation of Mystics. They were known as Lapis. Incredibly intelligent, persuasive, and physically strong, they could sniff out a liar from a mile away.

But he wasn't satisfied. Next, he fabricated the Mystics known as the Verdants. They were blessed with earth-based abilities, and telepathy with animals. He gave each generation a separate region to live in amongst their own people and nurture their gifts. Still, it wasn't enough. Wanting to replicate the Verdants, he formed the Scarlets, who could shapeshift into different human forms. As the Scarlets adapted and their abilities grew, they began to create illusions and trickery. This wasn't what Irus had planned, so he tried to balance this by making the Golds. Their abilities involved healing, aura-reading, and empathy. They were the kindness to the Scarlet's cruelty.

I'd forgotten that Scarlets had developed the skill of illusion and were not created with it. After all, it's what most of us knew them for. I wondered what other traits could be learned, and I shivered at the thought.

Irus's younger sister Kayja, Goddess of Travel, begged him to let her make her own creation. The two siblings were close, so he agreed, and they decided they would rule the Mystics together, and she created her own strong beings. Being the middle child, she wanted to prove herself to be as talented as her brother, but she was more adapted to telepathy and telekinesis. And so the Silvers were born. Kayja and Irus worked together to guide their Mystics into the path of light, doing good for the world.

I shifted at seeing the words "*Silvers were born*" as if my blood was on display for everyone to see.

And then there was Lethos, God of Shadows. Jealous and angry that no one ever paid him much attention, he plotted against his family. When he asked his siblings if he could create Mystics of his own, Irus laughed in his face. Kayja took pity on him and cut out a sliver in each region so he could make his own race. He did his best to match their creations, but none of his people had any abilities. They were known as the Commoners. Lethos was not strong enough to create the beings that would be his family's undoing, and he fled out of shame, never to be seen again.

I closed the book, somewhat comforted by the familiar story. I stared out my window, thinking. Never in my wildest dreams did I expect to end up in one of the Mystic regions so very far away from my home. I slipped the necklace over my head and let the cool metal fall against my skin.

With the memory of my family fresh in my mind, I promised myself I would do whatever it took to destroy the ones who took them from me. Even if that meant serving the Starr brothers.

CHAPTER 6

"Please let it be a dream," I said with my eyes still closed. "Please let it be a dream." I opened one eye and my heart fell. I wasn't back home in my tiny bedroom. Opening the other eye, I sighed as a beam of light peeked through the window, lighting a small path through the room. Just like at home, I watched the little dust motes dance in the beam of light and took some comfort in the familiar habit. I had always been an early riser. Not only was I fond of watching the sunrises, but picking the pockets of people on their way to work usually resulted in more profits for me.

I pulled the book of stories my dad packed me off my chest, sat up, and placed it on the bedside table. I hadn't meant to fall asleep with my clothes still on, but once I was alone last night with a full stomach, exhaustion settled into my bones, and I knocked out before finishing the story I had been reading.

As I stepped into the large bathroom, the lights automatically turned on by themselves and I froze mid-step.

Were Mystics so lazy that they couldn't even turn on their own lights? Shaking my head, I focused on the freshly folded towel sitting on the counter. Neatly placed on top was a note with my name written in delicate letters. I unfolded the note, and quickly realized this was my list of chores for the day.

1. *Clean and makeup mine and Jayce's room and take the laundry to be cleaned.*
2. *Inform Anthony Bogg that I will not be attending his event this evening.*
3. *Sweep the main floor and the elevator.*
4. *Polish the Grand staircase, and sweep the service stairwell. And if you haven't already...take a shower and always remain presentable.*

I rolled my eyes and tossed the note aside. I pulled my dusty clothes off and tossed them into a pile on the floor. Grabbing a towel, I walked towards the clear glass walls of the bathroom, looking for the shower. I tried to push the glass open, but it didn't budge. I tried again and again in different spots, but the only thing I could show for my effort was a trail of dirty fingerprints all over the glass.

Naked and frustrated, I slammed my hand against the glass. "Where's Alice when you need her?"

"Hello!" Alice popped up out of nowhere. I jumped back, covering my body immediately with the towel.

"What the heck?" I yelled. "Haven't you heard of a thing called privacy?"

She kept smiling, tilting her head like she was confused. "You called for me, so I'm here to assist you."

Adjusting the towel a little tighter around myself, I said, "I was just trying to take a shower."

"Oh yes, I forgot to mention last night, most of the house is voice-activated, like me. You just have to ask for what you want."

"Oh, okay. Well, you can leave," I mumbled, feeling extremely uncomfortable with her pixel eyes staring at me.

"Have a good day." She nodded once and disappeared. I let out a sigh of relief. It was definitely going to take a while for me to get used to the way things ran around here, and I made a mental note to be careful of saying Alice's name out loud.

I turned to the glass doors feeling like an idiot, and said, "Open." A panel of glass slid out of the way, allowing me access to the shower. Placing my towel on a hook, I looked up at the nozzle hanging from the ceiling. "Uh, turn the water on...hot water?" I quickly amended. I was in no mood to be doused with freezing water.

Again, the technology obeyed my command and a stream of rain fell from the ceiling. "Woah." It was nice being in control of something for once, no matter how little. Even in my wildest dreams, I would have never imagined that the Mystics had this kind of tech.

Once I'd scrubbed the last remnants of home from my body and my skin was flushed, I asked no one in particular to turn off the shower and sure enough, the water stopped.

"I could get used to this." The moment the words left my mouth I felt guilty. Sure, living here was much nicer than I expected, but I needed to keep my head on straight, find my brother, avenge my family, and destroy the Mystics.

I grabbed the towel, dried off quickly, and tied my hair into a braid. The clock read 5:30am. If I was ever going to get through my to-do list and still have time to do some snooping, I needed to get going.

I swung the double doors of the dresser open and rolled my eyes. An array of beautiful dresses was lined up in front of me. Did they really expect me to clean in a gown? Turning back to the bathroom, I grabbed my old, raggedy clothes, brought them up to my nose, and coughed.

Gross.

Normally I wouldn't care, except in this region, I'd stick out like a sore thumb in what used to be my favorite outfit. I needed to be invisible without using my abilities to do the dirty work for me. If anyone here found out what I could do, I'd lose my dad and my brother.

I discarded my clothes and went back to the dresser, opening all the drawers. There had to be something in here that wasn't totally out of the realm of possibility. In the bottom drawer, thankfully, I found something my speed. Grabbing a simple push-up bra, a black top with long, flaring sleeves, and dark shorts, I quickly got dressed. The top fit my body like a second skin and the stretchy material was light and comfortable. The shorts, on the other hand, were a bit too tiny for comfort, but they were flexible and easy to move around in.

Slipping on the pair of tennis shoes that were left for me by the door, I couldn't help but smile. It had been years since we were able to afford shoes that actually fit me. I had no idea how they knew my size in everything, which was actually kind of creepy, but I knew they all had their ways.

Looking at myself in the mirror, I was shocked at how different I looked. My figure was accentuated in all the right places and the hot shower had left a natural blush on my cheeks. With my dark braid sitting on my shoulder, I smiled at how much I looked like my mother.

"I guess it's time to get to work," I let out a heavy sigh. How anyone thought it was truly a reward to serve the Mystics was beyond me. Having nicer clothes and food had its perks, and I could see the appeal, but it was all an illusion to mask how Mystics treated Commoners.

I grabbed my to-do list from the bathroom and made my way out the door and down the hall to the stairwell. Starting with their rooms seemed liked like the best course of action. It would allow me to learn more about the Starr brothers and maybe even find something I could use against them. But how was I supposed to know if they were awake yet? I was well aware that most people didn't rise with the sun.

As I reached the fourth floor, I paused on the landing, not sure if I should go up to their rooms yet. "Alice?" I said to the empty stairwell

"How can I help you Willow?" she said from behind me.

Turning to face her I asked, "Do you know what time the Starr brothers wake up?"

"Jayce is already in the training arena this morning and Aaron asked to be woken up today at eight."

I was expecting both of them to sleep half the day away, and was surprised to learn that Jayce had already started his day.

"I guess I could start with Jayce's room." I frowned and looked at my list.

"Anything else I can help you with?"

"Mmm...yeah. Do you know who Anthony Bogg is?" Her head moved from one side to the other as she stared at me.

"Anthony Bogg, twenty-two years old, a painter by trade, and throwing a gallery party tonight at his penthouse located-"

"Okay, thank you," I interrupted her. "I don't need his whole life story. I just need to tell him...wait, can you look up everyone in the Scarlet region like that?" Hope bloomed in my chest that she might be able to help me find Eli.

"Not everyone is listed. Some prefer privacy. But if they've opted into the network, I can find them."

My heart felt like it was going to beat out of my chest and it took all of me not to grab her and demand she look up my brother.

"How about Elias Knight?" My tongue stuck to the roof of my mouth as nerves took hold of me. The thought that I might be able to see my brother again so soon after arriving here seemed impossible.

"Hmm, it doesn't look like he's listed."

My heart fell into the pit of my stomach. Of course Eli wasn't listed. I should've known better than to get my hopes up.

"But he does check into a bookshop every morning." She smiled and folded her hands in front of her. "Will that be all?"

I was about to ask her which bookshop he checked into when a warning bell went off in the back of my head. I wasn't sure how much I should rely on her. For all I knew, she was reporting my every move and every request back to Aaron and Jayce. If I was going to accomplish anything here, I would need to play my cards close to the chest. I needed to find Eli, but I also needed to be careful about searching for him.

"I'd like a map of the region so I can learn about my new home in case I'm asked to run any errands."

"That's a splendid idea, I will have that delivered to your room by the end of the day." She bobbed up and down on the balls of her feet.

"Thanks."

"Anytime." She blinked and vanished into thin air.

A small smile spread across my face. Eli may not be listed and I had no idea how many bookshops there were in the Scarlet region, but it was a start. If I could find him, then maybe, just maybe, we could find a way to put our family back together.

Looking down at the list in my hand I was reminded of why I called Alice in the first place.

"Shoot. Alice?"

"Yes?" She reappeared in the same spot.

"Anthony Bogg. How can I tell him that Aaron won't be attending his event tonight?"

She cocked her head to the side and smiled. "I just sent a message to his Alice informing him that Mr. Aaron won't be attending."

"*His* Alice?" I furrowed my brow.

"Yes, many households in the region have an Alice AI, just like me."

"So, if you can talk to other Alice's then why does Aaron need me to contact Mr. Bogg?" I looked down at my list and back up at her.

"You'll have to ask him." Her chipper voice and ever-present smile was starting to wear thin.

"Right," I said. There was no way in hell I was going to ask him anything- he gave me the creeps. "Thank you, Alice. That'll be all, for now." I started up the next set of stairs that led to Jayce and Aaron's rooms.

"Anytime."

Something didn't sit right with me. If the Mystics had all this technology to make their daily lives easier, then what did they need Commoners for? A chill ran down my spine at the thought. Whatever the reason, it couldn't be good.

Reaching the fifth floor, I opened the door and started toward Jayce's room, which was closest to the stairwell.

When I reached the door, there was a note taped to the front with my name on it.

"Let me guess," I mumbled. "Jayce has another list of demands for me." I sighed as I unfolded the piece of paper.

I do not require your services in keeping my room.

-Jayce.

I looked down the hall, up at the door and back down at the note. Was this some kind of trick? If I didn't clean his room, I'd be punished. But if he really didn't want me to serve him, then I might get in trouble for going against his wishes.

"Good morning!" A cheery voice rang out through the hallway. A kid was walking towards me, carrying white linens. He had sandy brown hair, combed neatly to one side, and was wearing a tidy outfit of black pants and a white shirt.

"Hi," I answered. "I'm Willow."

"You must be the new recruit! I'm Joseph. I was Chosen last year. I'm glad not to be the new guy on the block anymore!" My Gods, were they drugging the water here? How were they all so damn happy?

"Nice to meet you, Joseph. Could you help me? I need to find Jayce. Alice said that he was in the training arena. Could you point me in the right direction?"

Joseph shook his head. "You'll never find it on your own, not on your first day. Alice!"

She popped into existence next to me. "Yes?"

"You said Jayce was at the training arena this morning?" I asked.

"Yes."

"Can you take me to him?"

"Of course, right this way." She started down the hall away from the stairs.

"Nice meeting you!" Joseph shouted as I walked away.

"Um, Alice?" She turned back to look at me.

"Right, you don't like the elevator." Walking back in my direction she motioned for me to follow her into the stairwell. "It would be much faster."

"I don't mind," I shrugged as she started down the stairs.

Whatever game Jayce was playing, I had no interest in taking part. Not when I knew Aaron would jump at the chance to punish me for not completing my list. If Jayce didn't want my services, as he so nicely put it, that was fine by me, but he'd need to confirm it in person.

CHAPTER 7

Alice led me out of the back of the house and through a large garden. Giant trees towered over us, leaves dangling from their branches and swaying in the breeze. Birds chirped happily above, and I might have enjoyed my surroundings if I could forget about where I was.

I followed Alice along the stone path. It was hard to believe this place was real. Sure, we had beautiful, sweeping green hills back home, and there was no shortage of trees. But this was something else. It was as if nature was only just being held at bay, and without intervention it would take back the land in a matter of days.

A knot formed in the pit of my stomach as I tried to figure out the size of the Starr lands. Sneaking out of this place to look for Eli was going to be impossible if I didn't know how big this place was, or if someone was going to pop up out of nowhere at any second.

As we came around a bend, the trees started to thin ever so slightly, letting the soft morning sun touch my skin, and I noticed a large, nondescript building. It was half hidden by the trees, so I couldn't tell how big or tall it was, and there wasn't a single window from what I could see.

"This wasn't on the tour yesterday," I said, more to myself than Alice.

"There is a great deal that didn't make the tour yesterday. The Starr property is ten acres, though most of the property has been left in its natural state. There are some hidden gems on the property."

"I'd love to see it all sometime." I did my best to sound mildly interested instead of eager. I was impressed with how much the main house and this other building blended into the trees. If I squinted, it almost felt like I was in a lush forest away from civilization.

"I'm sure that can be arranged." She stopped in front of the door to the building and pressed a bunch of numbers on a data pad.

There was a soft click, and Alice pushed the door open. *What was so special about this place that they kept it behind a lock?* I wondered. The amount of tech the Mystics were keeping to themselves was hard to wrap my mind around.

I followed Alice inside, and my mouth fell open. I don't know what I was expecting, but it surely wasn't this. The entire building was one huge arena. The ceiling was at least twenty to thirty feet high, and completely comprised of glass. No wonder there were no windows on the exterior of the building.

I quickly understood why there was a lock on the door. Every type of weapon imaginable hung on the wall opposite from where I stood, and in the middle of the building I recognized a sparring ring. This one was much nicer than the ring back home, which was made of old crates and scraps of clothing. Off in another corner there were sparring dummies in various states of disrepair.

"Right this way, Willow." Alice turned right, and away from the wide-open arena. "Jayce is in the middle of a simulation."

She walked through another door into a small room. The wall opposite me was covered in tinted glass. On the other side, I could just make out someone who looked like they were fighting themselves.

"Hello, Jaxtyn," Alice's chipper voice pierced the silent room. "Willow would like a word with Jayce, can she wait with you?"

"Oh yeah, of course." The man Alice had called Jaxtyn swiveled in his chair and looked at Alice and I. "Is it urgent or can he finish up?" His sky-blue eyes met mine.

Alice turned toward me, and I realized they were both waiting for me to respond. "It's not urgent, but I also don't have all day." I waved the note Jayce had left for me, indicating that waiting around for him all day wasn't high on my list.

He looked back at the glass and down at the control in front of him. "I don't expect him to be much longer." I looked back at the person on the other side of the glass, who I assumed was Jayce, only to see him jump into the air like a cat and slash his way through the empty room.

"Wonderful," Alice chimed. "If you need anything else, you know how to find me." She smiled and disappeared without another word.

I waited patiently for a minute or so, and then glanced at Jaxtyn, only to catch him staring at me.

"Is there something on my face, or do you usually just stare at people rudely?" I asked before I could stop myself.

"Sorry. You're new here, aren't you? Willow, was it?" He didn't seem to be bothered by my rudeness. After he spoke he turned back to the screen and pressed some buttons on the control panel in front of him.

"Yep. Just got here," I answered, not really interested in making friends.

Jaxtyn turned back to me with a winning grin. "Well, if you need anybody to show you around..."

"I'm good, thanks."

We fell into an awkward silence, and I felt myself shifting from foot to foot uncomfortably. Maybe I should make a friend. I had no idea how long I was going to be stuck here, and I could use an ally.

"So, how long have you worked for the Starr family?" I asked. As much as I didn't want to admit it, I was curious about Jayce and Aaron and why they would have chosen someone like me instead of the standout, perfect citizen.

"Since I was eight," he looked up at me with a small secret smile.

"Eight years old?" My eyes nearly fell out of my head. What kind of people made *kids* work for them?

"I'm kidding!" He threw his head back and laughed. "Jayce and I have been friends since we were kids."

"Ahh, so you weren't Chosen," I said catching on.

"Not in the way you mean, no. But sometimes I do feel like Jayce chose me to be his best friend."

"So, you're close to the Starr family, then?" I asked.

"I'm close to Jayce," he corrected me and turned away to make a couple of adjustments on the screens in front of him.

I took note that he made the distinction between being close to the Starrs, and close to Jayce. There was clearly some bad blood between him and the rest of the family. I wanted to dig a little into his statement, but I had to be careful not to press my luck.

Instead, I took a tentative step forward so I could see through the glass better. "I assume he isn't fighting thin air." I cocked an eyebrow as Jayce spun through the air and sliced his sword through an invisible foe.

Jaxtyn let out a soft chuckle as he ran a hand through his platinum blonde hair. "No, he's not."

"What is this thing?" I watched as Jayce pulled the sword from his hip and started swinging the blade like it was an extension of his body. The way he moved was smooth and practiced- not one step was out of place. He spun and ducked out of the way of his invisible foes, landed in a crouched position before leaping into the air, and dodged an invisible attack.

Jaxtyn pointed to the control panel in front of him. "This is our fighting simulator. You can pick any real-life setting to test your abilities and physical strength."

"So, what's he seeing?" I nodded toward Jayce. From where I was standing, I could only see blue pixels.

Jaxtyn's eyes brightened, and I got the impression he was excited to explain all of this to me.

"Beats me," he shrugged. "Jayce won't let anyone see his simulations."

"So why are you here?" I blurted without thinking. A pang of fear ran through me and I hoped Jaxtyn wasn't in the mood to teach me a lesson.

"You know, I often wonder the same thing." He leaned back in his chair and laughed.

"Oh erm, I didn't mean-"

"I'm kidding." He moved back to the control panel in front of him and made a couple of quick adjustments. "Jayce may be able to set up his own simulation, but he needs someone to monitor the output. I might not be able to see what he can, but I can make adjustments if it's too easy or too hard."

"So what did you just do there?" I pointed to the screen he'd just pressed.

"You said you didn't have all day, so I made things a little more challenging," he shrugged. "He should be done in about sixty seconds." He looked through the glass and back at the console in front of him. "Make that thirty seconds."

Jayce moved almost too fast for me to keep up as he kicked, sliced, punched, and spun through the air. Whatever Jaxtyn added to the simulation, it was clearly making Jayce work harder than he was a moment ago.

"How is this better than fighting a real person?" I

furrowed my brow. It seemed pointless to fight against the invisible when there was plenty to fight right here in the physical world.

"The simulation goes beyond physical power." He pushed away from the screens and looked up at me. "It tests you emotionally, intellectually. Makes you fight against your loved ones or your deepest, darkest fears. It forces you to use every ability you have in your arsenal."

I looked back at Jayce and wondered what deep, dark fear he was battling against. He came from privilege, and he was a Mystic. What shadows and monsters could he possibly have?

"And if that's not enough, we can also introduce targets that are made to handle any weapon you can think of."

"What's the point of a weapon, when your abilities are the best defense against an enemy?" It never even occurred to me that a Mystic would take the time to learn how to defend themselves without using their abilities. It seemed like a lot of extra effort when their abilities would do the trick ninety-nine percent of the time.

"Some Mystics believe that's all they need." He gave me a crooked smile and shrugged.

"But Jayce doesn't."

"Doesn't what?" A deep, slightly out of breath voice made me jump.

"Oh! Umm..." His eyes caught mine and I quickly looked away.

Sweat glistened along his forehead and arms. Not only

did I hate myself for noticing, but I also felt like I was intruding.

"I was just telling her that some Mystics prefer to get their hands dirty." Jaxtyn leaned back in his chair with his arms over his head.

"Yeah, and some like to get off on torturing others." Jayce kicked at the chair and Jaxtyn almost fell over.

"Oh come on, it wasn't that bad."

"Next time, it's you in the box." He pointed toward the now empty room. "We'll see if you're still smiling after a round or two."

I cleared my throat and two pairs of blue eyes turned on me.

Jayce examined me carefully, and the intensity of his gaze made me feel like he could see right through me. "Did you need something? I assume you aren't ignoring your tasks just to chat with Jaxtyn on your first day."

"Could you blame her?" Jaxtyn winked at me, and I wished I could disappear into the floor.

I had to bite the inside of my cheek to fight back the retort on the tip of my tongue. "You left me this." I held out the note to him.

"And?" he asked without looking at it.

"I wanted to make sure it was you who left it and not some practical joke that ended up with me being tortured till dawn." My heart began to race, and I started to second guess my decision to come down here.

The smirk he'd be wearing since he finished in the simulation fell from his face as if I'd slapped it off of him.

"I understand." He folded his arms over his chest. "I did

leave the note, and as long as you serve in this house, I will ask that you respect my wishes and leave me to my privacy."

"Fine by me," I said as I nodded and started to back out of the room. The less I had to do for him the better. If only Aaron was the same.

"One more thing, Ms. Knight."

"Yes?" Fear prickled through me. I knew I shouldn't have come down here. He was probably going to give me a list of other tasks to do.

"No one will be torturing you while you serve in the Starr household." His eyes held mine and I could see that he meant it. But just because he wouldn't hurt me didn't mean others wouldn't jump at the chance.

"Tell that to your brother," I said under my breath.

The muscle in his jaw flexed and his lips formed a hard line. He could say nice things all he wanted, but there was no way he would go against his brother. Yesterday was proof of that.

"Was there anything else?" he asked, changing the subject.

I shook my head.

"Then I suggest you get back to work." He turned away from me as if he couldn't be bothered to wait until I left before he continued with his training.

"It was nice meeting you, Willow," Jaxtyn said as I made my way across the small space.

"You too." I gave him a small smile as I reached the door. As far as I could tell, he was the complete opposite of Jayce, and I wondered how someone who seemed so relaxed and easygoing could be friends with Jayce, who acted like every moment was life and death.

I made my way back into the main part of the arena feeling a little lighter. At least I wouldn't have to clean up after Jayce. It wasn't much, but I'd take what I could get. As I reached the exit, my stomach rumbled, and I immediately thought of the fresh bread from last night.

As I made my way back into the garden, I decided to head to the kitchen since I'd already knocked two things off my list for the day. Maybe living here wouldn't be so bad.

CHAPTER 8

I was wrong. Living here was going to be the death of me. Every inch of my body hurt, including my fingernails that were stained brown from the staircase polish. I didn't finish everything on my list until the sun had long since dipped below the horizon, and by the time I made it to the kitchen there were only a few scraps left. Honestly, I didn't mind. What Mystics considered scraps was far better than any of the food I used to steal back home.

I made my way to my room, already dreading the fact that I would have to wake up tomorrow and do this all over again. I looked down the hall at the door leading to the stairwell, and I groaned. As much as I hated the death box, I was in no mood to climb three sets of stairs right now.

Pressing the button on the wall in front of me, the metal doors slid open with a cheerful *ding!*

To my surprise, it wasn't empty. Jayce stood in the middle of the elevator in slim black pants and a deep blue button-up shirt that brought out the color of his eyes. The top button of his shirt was undone at the collar, exposing the hollow of his throat, and I hated myself for noticing.

"Hello, Ms. Knight." His eyes met mine as I nodded and gave him a small tight-lipped smile.

Shuffling onto the elevator, I felt like a woodland creature who reeked of sweat and wood polish. I pushed the button for my floor and moved to the opposite side of the elevator.

"I hope you had a good first day." He leaned against the wall and placed his hands on the rail behind him as the doors closed.

"Just peachy," I said, taking a breath and folding my arms across my chest. There was a citrus smell in the air mixed with something warm like vanilla and cedar that was oddly comforting.

"You really weren't happy to be Chosen, were you?" He edged a little closer to me and I realized he was the one who smelled like a spring morning wrapped in an autumn afternoon. He cocked his head to the side as he waited for me to answer.

"Would you enjoy being forced to serve people who think they're better than you?" A short sarcastic laugh escaped my throat as I turned to him. I didn't care what the consequences might be for my attitude as I met his gaze. If he wanted to punish me for ruining his perfect little daydream that Commoners loved to serve, then so be it.

His eyes dipped down to my chest and his brow furrowed. "That's an interesting necklace you have there," he said, changing the subject.

I looked down. I hadn't realized that my mother's necklace had wiggled free while I worked. Grabbing the dog tags, I shoved them back under my shirt and looked away from him. "It was my mother's," I said reluctantly as the fuzzy edges of my abilities starting to surface.

"*Was* your mother's?"

My heart started to race, and I could feel the ball of anger that lived in my chest unfurl. How dare he even ask about my mother when it was Mystics like him that took her life? "Yeah, she was killed by Scarlets when I was a kid." I held his gaze as my abilities threatened to bubble over. I wanted to disappear. No, scratch that. I wanted to make *him* disappear.

His mouth fell open and a look of shock passed across his eyes.

The death-box let out another *ding!,* announcing my floor as the doors slid open. I marched out of the elevator without so much as a glance backward.

"I'm sorry," I heard him exhale as the door closed behind me. As I made my way down the hall to my room, I vowed I'd always take the stairs, no matter how tired I was. It wasn't worth an encounter with either of the Starr brothers.

Opening the door to my room, I walked inside and threw myself down on the bed. Letting out a groan, I took a deep breath and did my best to let go of the rage that was swirling in my chest. Jayce wasn't worth a second thought. I had bigger fish to fry, after all.

Closing my eyes, I let my back relax into the soft mattress. I was sure that spending the day hunched over polishing the staircase had done permanent damage to my back. I stretched my arms over my head, and my hands hit something solid as my back popped.

I rolled onto my stomach and grabbed what looked like the tablets I'd seen all around the property. The moment my fingers touched the front surface it lit up, and there was a note from Alice on the screen.

Willow,

This tablet has been assigned to you so that you may be more efficient in your duties. Going forward, all requests from Mr. Aaron and Mr. Jayce will show up on this tablet. The map you requested can also be found on the main screen.

Should you have any questions, you know how to find me.

-Alice

"The map!" I sat up with renewed excitement. I was expecting a paper map that I could mark up and tuck under my pillow, but this would make searching for all the bookshops in the region so much easier. There was only one problem. Okay, *two* problems if I was being honest. I had no idea how to use this thing, and even if I did, I had to assume the device was being monitored.

Ping!

The tablet chirped in my hands and another message popped up titled 'To-Do List'. Groaning, I let my head fall forward. I was in no mood to learn about what was required of me until I got a good night's rest. Besides, I wanted to start looking for all the bookshops.

"Alice?" I said sitting up and scooting to the edge of the bed.

"Hello, Willow." Alice appeared in front of me, just as chipper and perky as ever. "I see you got the tablet."

"Yeah, about that." I held it out to her. "I have no idea how to use this thing."

"I can walk you through the basics." She took the tablet and sat down next to me.

With a swipe of her finger across the screen, the message with the to-do list disappeared. Turning the screen toward me, she explained where I could find any and all messages from the Starr brothers as well as the list of tasks that were expected of me. She also showed me how to message the other staff, including the kitchen, which I had to admit was the best feature so far.

She also showed me where to find the directory she mentioned before, with all the listed Scarlets. Again, I wanted to kick Eli for not listing himself. It would have made life so much easier for me.

Lastly, she showed me the map function and how to look up locations around the region. I let out a sigh of relief and said a silent thank you to the Gods. At least I wouldn't have to manually search for every bookstore that Eli might visit. I might still have a lot of work ahead of me, but this tablet would save me more than a few headaches.

"This thing is like a mini Alice," I said taking the tablet back from her.

She let out a lyrical laugh. "While it can be a great tool, it's a far cry from my capabilities."

"Is there anything else I should know?" I asked, clicking around on the screen.

"Make sure you charge it every night. You can place it anywhere on the nightstand and it will do the rest."

I nodded. I wasn't really sure what she meant, but setting the tablet on the nightstand every night seemed easy enough.

"Will that be all?" Alice asked.

"Yes, thank you," I said without looking up from the tablet, and she vanished from the room.

I clicked on the map the moment Alice was gone, and started to type bookshop into the search field. My finger hovered over the enter key for just a moment before clicking it. Going down this road was dangerous. Looking for the bookshop was one thing, but leaving the house and searching for Eli was another. If they found out I was sneaking out, or worse, caught me in the act, my dad would pay the price.

I knew I needed to be careful with my next steps, but at the moment I figured doing a simple search of bookshops was innocent enough. If they ever asked me why I was looking up shops, I could always lie and tell them I liked to read in my spare time. Not that I had any extra time to speak of.

In a fraction of a second, four different dots popped up on the screen and my heart started to race. Eli visited one of these every day, and though I didn't know which one yet, my heart already felt a thousand times lighter. It was only a matter of time before I'd be reunited with my brother.

I clicked on the bookshop closest to the Starr residence, and a picture of the shop and business hours appeared on the screen. The shop was small and looked more like a bakery that happened to sell books. Maybe that's why Eli went every morning, for the food and not the books, I reasoned.

Clicking through the rest of the list, I studied each shop, how far they were from the residence and whether or not I thought it could be the shop Eli visited.

"Only one way to find out," I sighed and decided that I would visit the second one on the list first. It wasn't the closest to the Starr residence, but it was in the heart of the region and seemed like the most likely candidate.

Now I just needed to memorize the route to and from the shop and find a way to sneak out of this place.

Ping!

The tablet beeped at me, and Aaron's name popped up on the screen. My heart kicked into overdrive and immediately I wondered if they'd discovered my plan.

Hesitantly I clicked on the message, and it filled the whole screen.

The staircase isn't up to standard. Do it again tomorrow and do it right. I won't ask again.

Blood rushed to my cheeks, and I had to fight the urge to throw the device across the room. I started to type back a response and tell him where he could shove the staircase polish, but the thought of seeing my brother stopped me.

Dealing with Aaron was a small price to pay if it meant I could be with my family again.

Taking a deep breath, I closed the message and went back to studying the map. I had no idea how long I stared at the screen in my hands, tracing out multiple routes and memorizing how many streets were in between each left and right turn. It wasn't until my eyes felt like sandpaper and the tablet flashed a warning that it needed to be charged that I finally put it on the nightstand.

Lying in bed, I stared out the window at the stars and I could almost pretend I was back home. As I watched the stars twinkle back at me, I let my thoughts drift to how much my life had changed in the last two days. No more stealing food, no more classes, no more Dad. My heart ached at the last thought, and more than anything I hoped he was doing okay without me.

Sleep pulled at me, and as I closed my eyes I could feel the smile forming on my lips. Tomorrow I would start the search for Eli. And with the thought of being reunited with my brother, I fell into a dream of when we were kids without a care in the world.

CHAPTER 9

Early morning light brushed across my face and my eyes fluttered open. The sky was still the light peach color that always accompanied the pre-dawn morning, and I was glad that I left the curtains open last night. Just because I was a morning person didn't mean it was always easy, especially after staying up all night researching every corner of the region.

Sitting up, I stretched my arms over my head and my nose wrinkled. I needed a shower. Between the wood polish and working my butt off all day I was in desperate need of some soap and water. Tossing the blankets back, I swung my legs out of bed and padded toward the bathroom.

As I crossed the threshold, the lights turned on, and I had to admit, it was a nice feature. I undressed, threw my dirty clothes in the corner and got into the shower. I wasn't sure how much time I had before Aaron and Jayce would be roaming around the house and wondering why I wasn't getting anything done off their list. The sooner I got out of the house, the better.

After scrubbing my skin red from trying to get all of the wood polish off of me and letting the warm water run through my hair, I realized I'd be covered in polish yet again today, but I didn't let that put a damper on my spirits.

Rushing out of the bathroom like I was already late for an appointment, I threw open the dresser and searched for something that looked a little more Mystic and a little less Commoner. If I was going to blend in, I'd need to wear their clothes.

I couldn't wrap my head around some of the more outlandish dresses with sparkly bits and several layers. So instead, I settled for a plain black dress with red stitching and a scoop neckline. The sleeves flared out at my wrist and the skirt just barely kissed the ground. It did very little to hide my figure, and I wondered what the Mystic's obsession with skin-tight clothing was. Didn't they want to be comfortable? Taking a quick look in the mirror, I was pleased to find that I didn't look like a Mystic or a Commoner. I was something else. A little elegance with sharp edges, and I had to admit, it was a good look on me.

I threw my hair into a tight bun on top of my head and looked at the tablet once more. I pulled up the map to the shop I'd selected last night, doing another quick study to make sure I knew where I was headed. Straight down the hill, past the port where I landed on my first day here, and then two rights and a left. I counted the streets in between each turn once more and then made my way out the door.

I slipped into the stairwell, grateful that everyone seemed so fond of the elevator. I'd only been here a little over a day, but in that short amount of time, I hadn't seen another person even glance in the direction of the stairs.

As I reached the last set of steps, adrenaline pulsed through me, and my heart started to beat faster. I could use my abilities and sneak out of the house unnoticed, but it was a huge risk to be using my gifts right under their noses.

Looking back up the way I'd come, I bit my bottom lip. I couldn't hear or see anyone. And this was probably the safest place in the entire house. I knew there was no way for me to walk out the front door without being seen by someone. I decided using my abilities was my only option.

I took a deep breath to steady myself, let down my walls, and allowed my abilities to take hold. A sense of relief washed over me now that I was no longer holding back, and I let out a small sigh of content. Looking down at my hands, I turned them over and watched as they vanished from the world along with the rest of my body.

For a second, I relished in the feel of my abilities and the raw power coursing through me. There were so many things the world had taken from me, but my blood made up for it in some ways. I took another deep breath as a chill ran down my back. My abilities were getting stronger with each passing day and with my birthday around the corner, I was nervous about what that might mean for controlling them. But that was a problem for another day.

"Focus, Willow," I said under my breath as I grabbed the handle and exited the stairwell.

I made my way down the hall, staying close to the wall, and crept along slowly. I might be invisible, but I could still draw attention with even the slightest noise.

"Right this way." Alice's chipper voice sounded up ahead and I froze halfway down the hall.

I held my breath as Alice and a man I didn't recognize walked toward me. Rationally I knew they couldn't see me, but I couldn't help the fight or flight emotion bubbling up inside me.

"Do you know if Jayce will be joining us today?" the Mystic asked as they passed right by me and stopped in front of the elevator a few feet away.

"I'm afraid not, he's otherwise engaged today," Alice said as the doors slide open, and they disappeared.

As the doors to the elevator slid closed, I breathed a sigh of relief.

"Is someone there?" A deep voice I recognized sent chills down my spine.

I turned to look at where the voice came from. I was inches away from broad shoulders, blonde hair, and blue eyes.

Shoot.

I held my breath and pressed myself against the wall. Aaron was literally the last person I wanted to run into right now. His brow furrowed as he looked past me down the hall, then back over his shoulder. After a moment or two, he frowned and continued down the hall and up the staircase. His hand reached out to touch the banister, but he stopped himself as if it was covered in mud. He grumbled to himself as he went up the stairs and I could have sworn I heard my name.

Once he was out of sight, I continued on my way to the front door. I had misjudged the sleeping patterns of the household, apparently. I saw Joseph walking through the main hall carrying what looked like a basket of vegetables, accompanied by a well-dressed woman who must be Anne, the cook. As I waited for the to pass me by, I heard a door open close by, and one of the servants I hadn't met yet stepped out with a bucket full of cleaning supplies. She made her way to the windows and began wiping them down, pausing every now and then to inspect her progress. I kept moving, slowly, making sure I wasn't going to slam into someone while invisible, and it took me longer than I would have liked to make it out of the house. Looking over my shoulder to make sure the coast was clear, I cracked the door open and slipped out of the house. The moment the door shut behind me, I made a run for it down the long, steep driveway.

I had no idea how much time I would have, especially knowing the other servants were awake and already working. And I didn't want to waste precious minutes strolling the streets when I could be at the bookstore, looking for Eli.

Once I made it to the first street, I hid behind a tree and let the invisibility fade away. I couldn't wander into town and just reappear at the drop of the hat if Eli was there. They'd for sure lock me up and throw away the key.

Walking down the mostly vacant sidewalk, I noticed that no two houses were alike. Some had fountains in their yards, outdoor pools and I even noticed a skywalk connecting two of the houses. Or maybe it was just one house? There were some houses that were all white, while others were a mixture of colors and textures. None of the houses looked like they belonged next to each other. And to me, it looked hideous.

The autumn breeze swept over me as I turned down the first street. The crisp morning air still carried the sweet floral scent from before, but today it was mixed with something warm, like cinnamon. I looked up at the sky. Small wispy clouds moved silently above me as the sky started to change to a light blue. I let myself take a moment to feel the ambiance of the calm street. Birds chirped and the breeze rustled through the leaves that had started to change red and orange.

I sighed and continued on my way. Butterflies danced in my stomach as I turned down the second street.

"Almost there, Willow." I couldn't help the excitement that was building in me, and though I knew it was a long shot, I held onto the promise Eli and I made to each other when we were kids. That no matter what life threw at us, or how dim things seemed, we wouldn't let the system break apart our family. It seemed like an easy promise to make at the time, but ever since Mom died it felt like no matter how hard we all tried, we were destined to break it.

As I made the final turn, I noticed a brightly colored poster of a missing girl attached to one of the lamp posts. A small grainy photo of a young woman with long blonde hair and green eyes about my age smiled up at me. Her name was listed as Silvia, and she'd gone missing about a week ago. I hoped that she was found, but I knew from experience, most people who went missing never came back.

I continued down the main street in the center of town, making sure to stay alert. There were a few more people milling about the streets and starting their day. Walking toward me was a man wearing clothes that looked like they'd cost a year's wages, and instinct took over. As he approached me, I didn't get out of his way and let him knock into me. As we bounced off each other, I reached my hand into his pocket and sure enough, there were a few coins. He apologized and we both dusted ourselves off before making our separate ways.

I smiled to myself and tucked the coins into my bra. If I ever wanted a fighting chance of getting out of here, I'd need money, and today was as good a day as any to start saving for the future.

Reaching the bookshop, I couldn't help but feel excited, anxious and a tiny bit nervous. In the front window was another picture of the girl on the missing poster with a number to call if you had any information. I couldn't help but wonder who would look for me if I went missing. Mom was gone, Dad would have no idea if I went missing, and Eli didn't even know I was here. Time to change that. *Eli, here I come.*

I pushed through the front door and a tiny bell announced my arrival. The shop was small and cozy, with books covering every surface possible.

"Morning, Miss." An older man popped his head from around a shelf.

"Good morning." My voice cracked from nerves.

"Let me know if you need help with anything," he said, ducking back behind the shelf.

I took a few steps toward a table filled with books and pretended to be interested. Truth be told, I never thought I'd make it this far. Now that I had, I didn't know if I should just wait for Eli to show up, which he might not, or ask the old man if he knew who Eli was.

I picked up a book without really looking at it and flipped it over in my hand. *This is stupid,* I thought as I put the book back down. The longer I was away from the Starr residence, the bigger the chance someone would realize I didn't belong here.

"Excuse me," I peeked around the corner to find the old man rearranging a shelf. "I'm supposed to meet someone this morning, but I'm not sure I have the right shop. I'm looking for Eli, Eli Knight. He said he drops in every morning."

He frowned and shook his head. "The only regular around here is Libro." He nodded towards the counter at the tabby cat perched on the glass.

"You're sure? He's a little taller than me, dark hair-"

"Sorry, hun," he said before I could finish. "There haven't been any tall, dark strangers in here since I was your age."

"Alright, thanks." I gave him the best smile I could manage considering he'd just dashed my hopes.

Frustrated and discouraged, I made my way out of the bookshop and stood on the sidewalk. I knew I should probably head back before anyone noticed that I was missing, but a big part of me wanted to sit down on the ground and let them come looking for me. Deep down I knew the chance of getting it right on the first try was slim, but I still held onto the hope that I'd find Eli today.

A man across the street laughed so hard it scared the birds away and caught my attention. He was leaning against the wall, wearing a white shirt with some sort of red logo on the breast. He was chatting and laughing with another man, who also wore a white shirt with the same red, 'L' shaped logo. It seemed familiar, but I couldn't quite place where I'd seen the logo before. Maybe in school, I thought as someone I recognized crossed their path. Jayce.

Oh no, no, no.

I dipped behind one of the planters outside the bookshop and watched as he approached an alley. He looked both ways like he was checking to make sure no one was watching and then made his way into the alley. Where was he going, and why was he acting like he didn't want to be followed? Crouched behind the flowers, I made sure no one was paying any attention to me as I slipped into my invisibility.

Crossing the street, I chased after him. If Jayce had a secret, maybe I could find a way to use it against him.

CHAPTER 10

I made my way into the alley, and immediately the fragrant stench of garbage and ale assaulted my nose. It was a far cry from the sweet floral smell that permeated the rest of the region. Jumping over a puddle, I noticed a stream of liquid ran down the middle of the alley, and I did my best to avoid it. Jayce didn't seem to mind the smell or the puddles as he stopped about halfway down the alley. Looking both ways again, his gaze lingered where I stood, and I was afraid my invisibility had somehow faded.

I looked down at myself and let out a sigh. Still invisible. I looked back up at Jayce and a small secret smile pulled at his lips before he knocked on the wall. Great, he's insane. I work for an insane person who loves the smell of trash and goes around knocking on walls.

A tiny slit appeared, and I realized that the wall was an illusion, and he had stopped at some kind of entrance.

Jayce reached into his shirt and held up a necklace that looked exactly like my mom's dog tags.

What the actual hell?

A heavy metal door swung open from the wall, and I stared in disbelief. I knew that Scarlets were gifted with illusions, but this was impressive. If I hadn't seen the door materialize with my own eyes, there's no way I'd suspect a secret entrance lay in front of me. I edged closed to Jayce and the secret entrance, careful not to make a sound. Positioning myself behind Jayce against the opposite alley wall, I strained my ears to listen.

A tall, lanky man leaned out of the doorway, one hand still on the handle. He reminded me of someone back home. Too thin because there was never enough food and dark circles under his eyes from working sunrise to sunset. But if he was a Commoner, what was he doing here, and how was Jayce involved in whatever he was up to?

Jayce exchanged a few hushed words with the man and handed him an envelope. Though I couldn't make out what he said, relief washed over the man's face as he gripped the envelope to his chest. I tried to look past the two of them and into the room beyond. The only light seemed to be coming from a candle or lamp somewhere in the room, and it was impossible to see even a few feet beyond the door.

What is this place? I wondered as I hovered behind Jayce.

Jayce's head whipped in my direction and I swear it felt like my heart stopped. He looked around me and then straight through before turning back to the man in the door. I let out a shaky breath and tried to get myself to relax. Any little move could spook him and I wanted to figure out what the heck he was doing here.

"You won't get a better chance," Jayce said under his breath. "You must leave a week from today, at twilight."

"I understand," the man whispered.

"Once you reach the coordinates, someone will be there to take you the rest of the way."

"How can we thank you?" The older man looked like he was close to tears.

"Don't thank me yet, you have a long way to go." He clapped the man on the shoulder and nodded once. "Take care of yourself."

"And you." The man pursed his lips and nodded.

Without another word, Jayce started down the alley in the opposite direction from the bookstore. The man watched Jayce walk away for a moment then closed the door. The moment the door clicked shut, the illusion fell back into place and it looked like an old alley wall once more.

Clearly this place was meant to be a secret, but why? What did this man, or Jayce for that matter, have to hide? And why did Jayce have something that looked a lot like my mother's necklace? I let my invisible hand graze over the surface of the invisible door. I couldn't help but sigh at the irony. I guess Jayce and I both had something to hide.

Without telling myself to do so, I started to follow him.

When he reached the cross street at the end of the alley, he made a left and I jogged after him. As I reached the street, I turned left and followed a few feet behind him. The few people who were already running morning errands gave Jayce plenty of space. As he walked toward people, they would either cross the street or duck into the nearest shop. Jayce didn't seem to notice, or if he did, he didn't pay them any attention.

Clearly, I still had a lot to learn about the Starr family if everyone else had the good sense to steer clear of Jayce. But if I was being honest, it only made me more curious. Why had the man in the alley looked at Jayce like he was one of the Gods, here to save him? Everyone else seemed to be terrified of him. It just didn't add up.

Jayce stopped at the next intersection, and I realized we'd reached the street that led up to the house. He looked to his left and then out of nowhere turned right and crossed the street. I wanted to keep following him, but I also needed to get back to the house before anyone noticed I was missing. I stood on the edge of the pavement, watching Jayce walk further and further away, and decided to let it go. For now.

Whatever Jayce was up to, I was determined to get to the bottom of it and get some answers about the door, and my mother's necklace. I made a mental note to take a more in-depth look into Jayce's schedule when I got back. If he had a habit of leaving the house in the early mornings, then I just might have to make it a habit as well.

Reluctantly, I made my way back to the Starr residence. The morning air was no longer cool, and beads of sweat began to drip down my torso beneath the heavy fabric of my dress. I fiddled with the necklace hidden beneath my dress, my thoughts swirling around Jayce, the necklace, and my mom. Everything about me being chosen seemed fishy, but now I was starting to think it was for a reason, and that terrified me.

Tracing the symbol on the necklace, I recalled what Jayce said last night when he noticed I was wearing the necklace. That couldn't be a coincidence, could it? There was something about the symbol that was connected to Jayce and my mom, but how was that even possible?

I couldn't help but wonder if Eli knew what was so special about Mom's necklace. Or if Mom or Dad had ever mentioned anything to him. It's possible it was just a Mystic thing, but then why would Jayce be sneaking around? There was one thing I was certain of- I needed to find Eli and get some answers.

Reaching the front door of my temporary home, I reached for the handle and froze. I couldn't just open the door and walk in while I was still invisible. Surely someone would notice the door opening by itself. But I couldn't just rematerialize and walk into the house either. What if someone saw me and wondered where I was coming from? I'd been so preoccupied with escaping, that I hadn't given much thought to how I was going to sneak back in.

I decided to give the back door a shot. At least it was glass and I'd be able to see if anyone was around. Jogging around the side of the house I almost ran right into Jaxtyn. I swerved around him, but he stepped on the edge of my dress and I tumbled into the grass, while he caught himself before hitting the ground.

"What the hell?" Jaxtyn righted himself and kicked the stone pathway. "This is why I hate mornings," he grumbled.

I picked myself up and left quickly. I couldn't wait around to be discovered. I made it around the back of the house, my heart pounding in my chest and my ears ringing from holding my breath. I hadn't had a close call like that in years. Now was not the time to slip up, especially not right in front of Jayce's childhood friend.

Once the coast was clear, I let out my breath. *Get it together, Willow,* I chanted to myself. I looked through the back door and I didn't see anyone, so I opened it as silently as possible. I slipped back into the house, and a chill ran down my spine. That was too close for comfort.

The access stairwell was just a few feet away when I heard Alice's sing-song voice coming toward me. I bolted for the door and ran up the stairs two at a time. Thankfully, I made it back to my room without running into anyone else. Heart racing and out of breath I closed the door behind me and sank to the floor. Today had seriously gone sideways. No Eli, Jayce in the alley, and almost outing myself. I was going to need a better plan going forward.

Getting to my feet, I pushed my abilities into the corner of my mind and let the invisibility fade away. Out of the corner of my eyes, I caught a glimpse of myself in the mirror as I materialized. I hated having to hide who I really was. It was like swimming against a current. I could never rest, and it was always a struggle to keep my abilities from overtaking me.

As I slipped out of the dress, cool air brushed against my sticky skin. I had no time for another shower, so I put on my Commoner clothes, grabbed the tablet off the nightstand, and clicked on the to-do list.

1. Clean the staircase again.

2. Make up mine and Jayce's room.

That was interesting. Aaron didn't seem to know that Jayce had asked me not to clean his room.

3. Clean the guest suites.

I groaned at the rest of the list. Based on how long it took me to finish the stairs yesterday, I needed to get started now if I had any chance of finishing everything before midnight.

I guess that meant no breakfast today. Good thing I was used to not knowing when my next meal would be. Replacing the tablet on the nightstand, I made my way out of my bedroom and up the stairwell to Aaron and Jayce's floor.

As I started down the hall, I noticed there was a note taped to Jayce's door once again. The tiny piece of paper starred back at me- my name printed in scrawling letters.

Why did he insist on leaving me notes when he could just send me a message on the tablet, like Alice said he would? I couldn't decide which was worse, the obnoxious *ding!* of the tablet every time Aaron added something to my list, or the notes Jayce left that felt like little bombs waiting to catch me off guard.

I was starting to understand why the woman who brought me here seemed wary of Jayce. He did things differently and clearly had secrets- two things that always made people feel uncomfortable. I should know.

Plucking the note from the door, I sighed as I unfolded the paper.

I require your assistance in the arena tonight after you've completed your tasks.

Well, isn't that perfect, I thought. Now I wouldn't need to come up with an excuse to ask him some questions. Sure, I couldn't ask him outright why he was in town today at some secret location with a necklace that looked just like mine. But I could try to find out more about the necklace and see what he has to say about it.

I stuffed the note into my pocket and made my way to Aaron's room, which of course was a complete and utter disaster just like it was yesterday. I swear he was making a mess just to torture me. Looking at the laundry that was thrown over every surface, I sighed. *The sooner you get this done, the sooner you can dig into Jayce and all his secrets,* I told myself.

CHAPTER 11

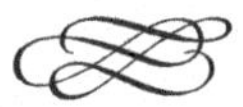

The sun was just starting to set, throwing an array of pinks and purples across the sky when I finished with the staircase. I looked down at my hands and sighed. They were covered in polish, again. And my lower back was killing me, again. I swear if Aaron made me do the staircase again tomorrow, I just might risk running away. I dropped my supplies off in one of the closets, and made my way to the kitchen for a quick bite before heading to the arena.

They'd cooked some sort of sweet bread today that filled the house with the most mouth-watering aroma. I thanked my lucky stars there was some set aside for me, along with a plate of fruit and a chicken leg. It wasn't much, but it was more than I ever could have hoped for a few days ago.

I spread some honey on the last piece of bread and popped it into my mouth. I could feel myself coming back to life. Sure, my back still hurt and I was in desperate need of a shower, but at least I wasn't hungry. I thanked the kitchen staff and made my way outside towards the arena.

The excitement of this morning bubbled back to the surface. I'd spent most of the day trying to think of a reason Jayce and my mom would have the same necklace. I came up with half a dozen scenarios, but none of them seemed plausible. From what I could remember about my mother, she had no reason to be associated with the Mystics.

As I reached the door of the arena, I pulled my necklace from inside my shirt and laid it on my chest. I wanted to give him the opportunity to mention it again, so I could try to glean something from him. I punched in the code Alice had given me earlier and the door clicked open.

The soft blue evening light cast a glow over the large open space, making it feel smaller. There was something peaceful about the way the trees hung over the glass roof, inviting only enough light to allow me see a few yards in front of me.

"I was wondering when you were going to make it down here." Jayce walked out of the shadows near the simulation room. A light sheen of sweat clung to his forehead and his eyes were bright and wild.

"Just finished for the day." I gave him a tight-lipped smile. What I really wanted to say was that some of us didn't have the luxury of being able to do whatever we wanted all day.

"I see Aaron is keeping you busy then." He moved into

a beam of light, and I was sure he wore the same crooked smile as this morning.

"You asked for my assistance?" I was in no mood to talk about Aaron or how busy he was keeping me.

"Jaxtyn mentioned you showed an interest in the simulator." He turned and motioned for me to follow him. "I thought it might be useful to teach you how to operate it."

"Why?" I blurted as I followed him toward the simulation room.

"Does it matter?" He looked over his shoulder and his icy eyes caught mine. If that's the way he looked at most people, I understood why they kept their distance.

"No, it doesn't," I said holding my own. Even if he seemed a little unhinged, I needed to play nice if I was ever going to get anything out of him.

"I'll be spending most of my time here, and I'd like for you to document the results." He opened the door to the simulation room, and I followed him in.

"Isn't that why you have Jaxtyn?"

"He isn't available in the evenings." He sat on the edge of the console and folded his arms over his chest. His eyes dipped to my necklace for a fraction of a second and I knew this was my opportunity.

"Listen, about last night." I reached for the dog tags and looked down at them. "I was just taken off guard." I looked back up at him and tried for the whole sad and innocent act I'd seen plenty of my classmates put on for our teachers.

"I'm sorry about your mother." His eyes met mine

and all his hard edges fell away. Jayce really was a chameleon, shifting from one emotion to the next flawlessly. It made it hard to tell where you stood with him.

"You said it was an interesting necklace." I looked down at the triquetra symbol. "I don't know much about it, only that she..." I paused for dramatic effect. "That she always wore it."

He pushed himself off the console and stepped toward me. "May I?" He held his hand out and I nodded.

His fingers wrapped around the dog tag and his thumb moved over the symbol. "The triquetra is traditionally known for family, unity, and protection," he quoted the line I'd heard a million times. He let go of the necklace and took a step back. "There are some who believe it's a relic of the Silvers, a token to prove some survived the slaughter all of those years ago."

My heart leapt into my throat as my blood turned ice cold. "That's impossible," I managed to squeak out.

He shrugged, "You're probably right. But it doesn't stop people from believing what they want to." He pressed a few buttons and the screens in front of us came to life.

"Shall we?" He started toward the door that led to the simulation room.

"Err, you want me to go in there?" I took a step backward. This was going horribly wrong. I was supposed to be learning more about him, not the other way around.

"The only way to understand how this works," he motioned to the simulator, "Is to experience it for yourself."

My eyes widened and my heart felt like it had fallen into my stomach.

"But I don't have abilities," I said, trying my best not to panic. "What would be the point?"

He raised one eyebrow as he leaned against the door frame. "The simulation isn't just for honing your abilities. It's also meant to discover and evaluate your biggest strengths." He looked me up and down and the hairs on the back of my neck rose. Something about the way his eyes scrutinized me sent alarm bells off in my head. It was like he was searching for something.

"I don't need a machine to tell me what my strengths are," I argued as my abilities hummed just beneath the surface.

"Fair enough," he held up his hands in surrender. "But you still need to understand how it works."

I took another step back and shook my head. I was sure he thought I was scared of the simulation, but really, I just wanted to keep my head on my shoulders. If he found out that I wasn't a Commoner... I didn't have to imagine what they would do to me.

"You have nothing to worry about." He picked up on my hesitation. "You can't get hurt. Once the projection makes a killing blow, the session will end."

"I don't think I'm the best candidate to help you, maybe Alice-"

He raised his hand to silence me. "I must insist, unless you want me to report to Aaron that you snuck out of the house today."

My heart felt like it was going to pump right out of my

chest and my cheeks flushed red. How the heck did he know?

"I don't know what you're talking about." I folded my arms over my chest. I learned a long time ago never to admit to something when they didn't have solid proof.

He closed the gap between us. "You don't want to play this game with me." He kept his voice low, and I had to fight to maintain eye contact.

"Whatever, let's get this over with." I pushed past him and towards the door, but his hand gently grabbed my shoulder, stopping me.

"If I told you not to do it again, it wouldn't make a difference, would it?" My eyes met his and I forced a smile.

"I don't know what you're talking about." I rolled my shoulder and his hand fell away.

"You need to pick a weapon." He pointed to the wide array of swords, shurikens, bows, and countless other pieces of equipment I've never seen.

I was drawn towards one sword in particular. Its deep purple handle had violet gems intricately woven in. A golden feather-shaped structure wrapped around the handle and as I picked it up, the lightweight sword balanced perfectly in my left hand.

Like magic, the golden structure tightened carefully around my hand for a better grip. At the simple thought of it loosening up, it obeyed. Turning my head towards Jayce in question, he stared at me blankly, not showing any emotion.

"Interesting. The sword picked you," he noted.

Throwing him a dumb look, I rolled my eyes. "I picked the sword. What are you talking about?"

"Some weapons have a magical entity attached to them. You don't realize it has that entity until the weapon ends up in a certain Mystic's, or apparently Commoner's, hand." He cocked his head to the side as he studied me. "It's unheard of for a Commoner to have any effect on the magic in a weapon."

"Oh," I murmured, not knowing what else to say. "Strange," I shrugged and turned away from him. I needed to stay in control if I was going to have any chance of coming out of this alive.

"You're different, aren't you, Willow?" It sounded more like an accusation than a question.

"We are all different in our own ways," I diverted.

"Very true," he smirked as if I'd confirmed something for him. I wanted to smack the smile off of his face.

"So are we doing this or not?" With my heart racing and my abilities near to the surface, I was ready to get some aggression out.

"Ready when you are."

I sauntered into the simulation room and the doors shut behind me. I was surprised that there weren't any blue pixels like I'd seen through the glass. Instead, a woman formed in front of me. Her dark hair cascaded down her back like a waterfall, and she held a sword identical to my own. Her violet eyes met mine and I was sure my heart stopped in my chest.

My breathing quickened, and I couldn't slow it down

as she came towards me. "No," I murmured. "No." I couldn't fight my mom.

"Remember, it isn't real," Jayce's voice came through the speaker system.

I took a deep breath, focusing on my next move. Failing wasn't an option, not with Jayce on the other side of the door watching me.

My mom, or the simulated version of her, stepped forward, her blade slicing through the air. Startled, I dropped to the ground to avoid being hit. Rolling away from her, I got to my feet and gripped my sword. As blood pumped furiously through my veins, my abilities begged to be released. For once I didn't resist, and let a sliver of my abilities take control of the blade.

Instinct took hold and propelled me forward. Each time she tried to get the better of me, I countered with a blow of my own. I hated that it was my mom that I was fighting in the Mystics' simulation, when they were the ones who took everything from me, including her, and destroyed what was left of my family.

I focused on the projection in front of me, and her features started to shift, no longer resembling my mom. I wasn't sure who it was, and I didn't pay attention to the details. My sole focus was to destroy the embodiment of the people who killed my mother.

I ducked another blow, and a grin spread across my lips. She'd left herself wide open and I took the opportunity to head straight for her abdomen. She stood no chance.

As my sword entered her body, she vanished, and the simulation ended.

"That wasn't supposed to happen," Jayce's voice came through the speaker system. His words pierced through me as fear pulsed hot in my veins.

CHAPTER 12

The door to the simulation room thrust open, and every nerve in my body tensed. I wasn't sure if he knew I'd used a tiny bit of my abilities, or if he was just impressed that a Commoner was good with a sword. With my abilities still close to the surface, I had to fight the urge to let it take control. Once I showed my true colors, there was no going back.

"You killed the projection." Jayce stared at me, wide-eyed and confused. I couldn't read the emotion on his face, but since he hadn't tackled me to the ground, I did my best to stay calm.

Standing up straighter, I glanced down at the sword, and back up at Jayce.

Putting on the innocent act again, I shrugged as if it was no big deal. "My brother gave me sword training when I was younger." A memory of Eli teaching me how to hold a sword tugged at my heartstrings. I was so young, but his lessons stayed with me, even after he was taken. I practiced every morning to preserve his memory. I would be forever grateful for Eli teaching me how to defend myself.

"I don't think you understand." Jayce furrowed his brow and shook his head. "You outmaneuvered the projection and killed it." He said each word slowly as if he was explaining what happened to a child.

Frustration bubbled in my chest, and I had to fight the urge to tell him off. I understood perfectly what he was saying, but I couldn't come right out and tell him that when you have my blood a projection is nothing. Instead, I opted for a sugar-coated insult. "Is that supposed to be hard to do?"

"It's meant to be impossible, especially for a Commoner." He shook his head and his eyes crinkled at the corners as he laughed. I was surprised he wasn't offended or angry. He was actually laughing, and I felt a little of the tension leave my body.

"Well, maybe you Mystics are just too soft," I said testing my boundaries. With most people, it was easy to know where the line was, what buttons to push, and how far you could push them before they snapped. But with Jayce, I had no clue. One minute he was dismissive, the next he was apologetic. And so far, not once had he used his abilities on me like the other Mystics.

"Or maybe there's something different about you." His smile turned soft as he looked me up and down.

The blood drained from my face and washed away all my bravado. All I could think was that I needed to do damage control. "You could say that," I bent down and picked up the sword. "I grew up learning to fight instead of playing with the other kids." Holding onto the hilt I rotated the blade back and forth as I spoke. "I grew up learning how to take care of my dad, instead of the other way around." I keep my eyes on the blade instead of Jayce. There was something about the way he was looking at me that made me feel exposed, and I wasn't sure how I felt about that.

"It's always the hardships that make us stronger," he acknowledged. "Still, it's impressive." He reached for the sword, and I let him take it from me.

Did he just compliment me? I wondered.

"The simulation is designed to never lose," he continued to ramble, and I kept my mouth shut. The less I said, the better. "Each individual who enters the simulation is targeted with a unique scenario that preys on their insecurities." He looked around the room as if he was seeing his own defeats play out in front of him.

I couldn't help the smile that pulled at the corner of my mouth as I watched him pace around the room. He was talking out loud and waving the sword around, but it was clear he was talking more to himself than to me. As I watched him try to puzzle out what happened, I realized he didn't seem angry. In fact, he looked excited. I added curiosity to my ever-growing list of Jayce's traits, and then cringed. I wasn't supposed to be interested in learning more about anyone here. My focus was meant to be on my family.

He stopped pacing abruptly and turned toward me.

"We need to do more tests, and simulations, to try and figure out why you were able to beat it." His eyes met mine, wide with excitement, and I felt my mouth go dry.

My smile vanished at his words, and I realized I was making him just as curious about me as I was about him. I groaned internally. I needed to get out of this situation before he found out who I really was. I don't know what made me think I could actually be a servant in another region for a portion of my life. I couldn't even make it a week without someone getting curious about me and what I could do.

"If it's all the same to you, I'd rather not be an experiment on top of being a servant." I grabbed my arm protectively, trying to make myself look small so he would think twice about what he was asking of me.

"Aren't you curious about why you were able to defeat the simulation?" His brow furrowed as he took a step toward me.

I shrugged. "Curiosity is for the privileged." I held his eyes, willing him to let go of the topic. "For others, it's a death sentence."

My words seemed to have some effect on him, and he took a step back, and the excitement in his eyes dimmed. "You really don't trust Mystics, do you?"

"I don't trust anyone." The memory of him sneaking around this morning flittered through my mind. People who can be trusted don't have secret meetings in dirty alleys, hidden behind illusions.

"That's no way to live." He folded his arms over his chest and tilted his head to the side.

"Well, when you've had your mother killed right in front of you and your brother dragged off to join the Mystics, then you can talk to me about trust."

"You've been hurt, I understand that. But to go through life without trust seems lonely."

"How could you possibly understand what it's like to have everything ripped away from you, when you live here," I motioned with my arms. "And your family is still intact." Angry tears stung the back of my eyes, but I refused to show any weakness in front of him.

He stood up taller and his entire demeanor changed from conversational to defensive. "Do not presume to know me, Ms. Knight." His lips formed a hard line, and he closed the gap between us. "I've known horrors that would make your nightmares look like fairytales."

A chill ran down my spine and I had to fight the urge to shiver.

"If you're not interested in who you are then neither am I." He turned and walked out of the simulation room.

"That's it?" I followed after him. "You're not going to make me or threaten me again?"

"I don't make it a habit to force anyone to do something against their will."

"That's rich, coming from the guy who I'm here to serve."

He turned on me then and closed the gap between us. "And have I not excused you from the tasks that you were assigned to on my behalf?" His eyes bore into me like he wanted to burn a hole through my head.

I nodded, surprised by the proximity of his body to

mine. The soft citrus and vanilla of his cologne filled my nose and my words were lost on my tongue.

"You may not like being here, but that doesn't mean you can go around being disrespectful. You don't know me, and your lack of restraint is going to get you into trouble one day."

"Yeah, I've heard that before."

"I'm sure you have, but this time it isn't an idle threat."

I opened my mouth to tell him off, but he held his hand up to silence me.

"Enough of your rebuttals. I asked you here for a purpose. So, you can either help me or get back to polishing the staircase and folding laundry. The choice is yours."

He turned away from me and back to the console.

"If I help you, does that mean I won't have to deal with Aaron's list anymore?"

He turned to look at me, a smirk on his face. "I can't make any promises. Aaron is," he hesitated. "Well, let's just say he's more traditional, and has certain expectations of Commoners."

"But you don't," I said more as a statement than a question. The fact that he had yet to ask anything of me until now proved that he didn't operate like his brother.

"No, I don't," he said matter of fact.

I can't say that surprised me based on my time here so far, but I wasn't expecting to meet a Mystic with a conscience. If I played my cards right, I just might be able to make this work for me. "And if I say yes, I don't have to do any experiments?"

He rolled his eyes. "I'll leave that up to you. Should you change your mind, the offer stands."

"Alright, but I don't want to have to polish the staircase anymore."

"I'll see what I can do." He smirked and sat down at the console.

"So how does this all work?" I stepped up to the wall of screens. I wasn't one hundred percent convinced that this was a good idea, but at least it would allow me to learn more about him and how he might be connected to my mother. And if it got me out of some of my cleaning duties, I couldn't complain.

We spent the next couple of hours going over every setting, every option, and more than once I accidentally shut down the whole simulation. It's not that it was all that hard to figure out, there were just so many screens and scenarios to keep track of at any given time, and I already had enough on my mind without learning how to operate the simulation.

"I think we should call it a night," Jayce said after I shut down the machine for the third time in a row.

"Oh, thank the Gods," I groaned and my stomach rumbled.

"When was the last time you ate?" He eyed me.

"I had a quick bite before coming down here tonight."

"Come with me," he nodded for me to follow him.

As we I followed, he typed furiously into his handheld device. Crossing the wide-open floor, we made our way to the other side of the arena, and he pushed a door open.

"After you," he smirked, and I wasn't sure how I felt about him being so nice.

As I stepped over the threshold, I paused mid-step, shocked at my surroundings. Trees and gorgeous, blooming flowers surrounded the room. A cream-colored hammock was stretched between two trees to my left and above us, twinkle lights hung throughout the see-through ceiling. The flowers gave off a refreshing aroma and the tranquility of the room was relaxing, making me feel right at home. A wood table with cream-colored chairs sat off to my right, and a few of the kitchen staff were placing small plates of food out.

"You ready to eat?" Jayce smiled, blinding me with his teeth.

I nodded. "I keep being surprised by how big this place is," I said under my breath as I walked toward the table. "It's beautiful."

"It's my favorite place to go to when things get stressful," he admitted softly.

"Stressful?" I snorted. "How could anything get stressful for you?"

"You think you're the only one with a lot on their plate?" He raised an eyebrow.

"No, I just-"

"You just think you have the right to judge my life because it looks easy from the outside." He turned to face me, forcing me to take a step back.

My mouth fell open and then I snapped it closed. He was right, after all. I hated when people judged me when they didn't know anything.

"I didn't mean-"

He cut me off, "I think we both know what you meant." He motioned for me to take a seat. "As someone who has been misunderstood for most of her life, I'd hope that you'd learn not to judge others."

I wasn't sure what to say to that. What did he know about me or my life?

"You're right, your life does look easy from where I'm standing," I folded my arms over my chest. "You get to make your own decisions, you get to come and go as you please, you get to choose your destiny."

"How naive," he shook his head. "No one gets to choose their destiny."

"I refuse to believe that."

"Then I fear you may live a life full of disappointment." He turned away from me and took a seat at the table.

"Yeah well, I'm used to being disappointed," I shook my head and started heading back the way we came.

My whole body shook with anger. He didn't know a single thing about what it was like to have to fight for even the bare minimum.

"Freaking privileged Mystic," I grumbled as I shoved the door open into the arena.

I made my way through the arena and back into the house, and my abilities started to surface, bubbling up in my anger. As I reached the back of the house, the garden lights started to flicker. I paused at the backdoor and took a deep breath to calm myself. It wouldn't do me any good to let my anger get the better of me and reveal myself.

The lights in the garden flickered once more and

returned to a steady soft glow. I pushed the door open and walked down the hall, making my way into the service stairwell. As I made it to the second floor, my anger started to settle to a manageable smolder.

When I got to the third floor, I exited the stairwell and walked to my room. I'd been hungry before, but now all I felt was exhausted. Exhausted from all the work, exhausted from keeping my abilities under control, exhausted from Jayce.

"Hey!" a voice sounded down the hallway. The servant I had seen cleaning the windows the morning I snuck out was walking down the hall. I really wasn't in the mood to make friends.

"Hi," I said shortly.

"I noticed Aaron assigned the staircase to you. It's pretty tough work. I think I still smell the polish in my sleep," she wrinkled her nose as she said it, and I relaxed a little. A kindred spirit. "I'm Kerry."

"It's nice to meet you. Yeah, he's already had me do it over since he wasn't happy with my work. I didn't realize something that you step on had to be so clean all the time," I said, rolling my eyes.

Kerry laughed, and reached out her hand. "They sell this soap in the village. Jack does a run once a week to get supplies, or you can ask Alice if she has some in stock. It's the only thing that gets rid of the smell fully. Well, almost fully."

I felt a rush of gratitude towards the servant. Thank the Gods I had a way of getting rid of that smell.

"Can we not go into town on our own?" Would I be trapped in this house forever?

"We can, but we have an allowance from the Starr's that's handled by Jack, so it's easier to just get him to pick it up for us rather than having to go get permission from Aaron. He usually goes on Monday, so you missed this week's shop. "

I smiled at Kerry, a genuine one. "Thanks for the info. I'm going to get scrubbing." With an exaggerated eyeroll for dramatic effect, I stepped into my room.

I changed out of my work clothes and showered, using the soap Kerry gave me to rid myself happily of the polish smell. I dressed in the sweater my dad packed me and a pair of loose shorts. There was still a faint smell of cedar and moth balls on the sweater, and as I took a deep breath I could feel some of my control clicking back into place.

I laid in bed staring at the ceiling, practicing a few of the breathing exercises that had always helped keep me calm and keep my abilities in check. It was getting harder and harder by the day. I felt like a ticking time bomb and my birthday was the detonator.

Closing my eyes, I continued to focus on my breathing and started to relax each part of my body until I fell into a restless sleep.

CHAPTER 13

I stood in the living room of my home, but everything looked the way it did when I was a kid, fresh and full of life. I heard someone coming around the corner, their soft footsteps a memory on my heart.

"Mom?"

"Hey, Willow, would you do me a favor?" She turned around to face me, her violet eyes grasping mine. "What's going on, my meraki?" She furrowed her brows

The nickname I hadn't heard in so long made my heartache. Meraki was a word she learned from my grandparents. It was a long-forgotten language of our kind and it was hard for her to describe what it meant. But roughly, it translated to intense love and care for something or someone.

"You aren't real." I squeezed my eyes shut tightly.

"What are you talking about?" She gave me a warm smile and shook her head, "Anyways... I was going to let you know

your brother will be here any minute." My eyes widened in realization.

I was dreaming of the morning she died. "No, Mom, he can't come over," I said quickly. "We need to leave," I urged, grabbing her arm. It was soft and warm to my touch.

"Stop being ridiculous, Willow."

"Willow!" Eli's familiar voice shouted in excitement. His strong arms gripped me in a tight hug.

"No, this is all wrong!" I yelled, beginning to freak out.

"My meraki, you need to stay calm." Her pleading eyes made me want to listen.

"I can't go through your death again, Mom." My eyes teared up.

"I don't know what you are talking about, Willow. Here, have a seat. I'm right here, okay? Nothing bad will happen, I promise." I shook my head, pushing her arm away as she reached towards me.

"What's going on?" My dad walked inside, taking off his jacket.

"We need to leave!" I yelled. All the fear I had built up exploded around me. A boom shook the house, and suddenly I was in the closet, hiding with Eli. "No," I said slowly.

I could hear the boots coming down the hall and I didn't want to watch my mom die again. I couldn't.

Wake up, Willow.

Wake up.

PING!

The tablet on the nightstand chirped next to me, pulling me out of my dream. I'd never been more thankful for an unexpected wake up until I saw the message.

Penthouse, 10 mins.

I threw the tablet on the bed next to me and let my head fall back onto my pillow. I swear to the Gods, if this was about the staircase, I was going to lose my ever-living mind.

I threw the covers off me and padded into the bathroom. I would have loved to have taken a shower first, but a splash of water on my face was all I really had time for. I slicked my hair back into a ponytail and quickly threw on a pair of the tiny shorts I was starting to hate and a black top with short sleeves.

The tablet let out another chirp and I groaned. "Now what?" I picked the tablet off the bed and my to-do list popped up with double the amount of work. I immediately threw the tablet back onto the bed without looking at it. Today was already proving to be a crappy day and I'd only been awake for a few minutes.

I left my room and walked down the hall to the elevator. I didn't want to take the stupid thing, but I noticed the other day that the stairwell ended at the fifth floor. The only way to get to the penthouse was to take the elevator. It seemed odd that the stairs didn't go to the sixth floor, but nothing about this place really made sense to me anyway.

As I waited for the elevator, my nerves starting to get to me. What if Jayce told him I snuck out yesterday? Or what if he knew I was trying to find my brother? I'd been here less than a week and I already felt like there was a long list of things that could get me in more trouble than I cared to think about. I knew I wasn't cut out for this servant life, but I also knew how to get out of sticky situations. Rule number one of not getting caught, act like you have nothing to hide.

I let out a nervous breath as I got onto the elevator and pushed the button for the top floor. The death box lurched toward the sky.

At least the ride was short, and the doors slide open just a few seconds after they'd closed. "Here we go," I said under my breath.

Aaron was on the far end of the room looking out the window as the sun cast a golden hue across the landscape. If I wasn't so anxious about why Aaron had called me here, I might actually enjoy the view.

"You asked for me, Mr. Starr?" I said when he didn't acknowledge that I'd arrived.

"Jayce has requested I lessen your workload so that you may help him with his training." He didn't turn to look at me as he spoke. He paused, letting me sit in silence and wait for his decision.

"I'm afraid that won't be possible," he said, finally turning away from the windows. His eyes skated up and down my body and his nose wrinkled in disgust.

Shweed. I didn't look that bad.

He took a few steps toward me and cocked his head to the side. "Though my brother has always had a bleeding heart, it's out of character for him to ask for leniency on behalf of a Commoner." He studied me like a bird ready to swoop down on a dying animal. "What is it about you that makes him so curious?"

"I have no idea," I shrugged.

He smirked and took another step closed. "Oh, but I think you do."

My heart started to race, and my fight or flight kicked in, looking for a way out of here if this went south.

"I've done some digging on you. Last in your class, a recluse amongst your community, always in trouble with the law. And your family, well, they weren't exactly upstanding citizens."

"Don't talk about my family." My hands balled into fists at my side.

"Ahh, yes and there's that temper of yours." He circled around me, and my body stiffened. "So, it begs the question." I could feel him just behind my right shoulder and I had to fight the urge not to shudder. "Why were you Chosen when you don't meet a single criterion for the job?" He whispered against my ear, and I flinched. My abilities prickled across my skin and every nerve in my body screamed for release.

"How the hell would I know? I didn't even want to be Chosen."

"My point exactly." He grabbed my arm and whipped me around so I was facing him.

"Let go of me." I tried to rip my arm free, but he had a death grip on me. The look in his eyes told me I was in trouble.

"So why would Jayce make sure you were Chosen? Why would he request that you work for him in the arena?"

"Wait, what?" His words stunned me. *Jayce* made sure I was Chosen? *Why*?

"You said it yourself, he was there at the ceremony." He gripped my arm tighter and yanked me forward. "You think that's a coincidence?" His anger was starting to get the better of him and I couldn't understand why. What did he care if Jayce hand-picked me? What did it matter to him if I was Chosen? His laundry was still getting done and the staircase was polished. So what gives? Something about this whole situation didn't sit right with me. And even though I didn't understand why Aaron was angry, I had the same questions.

"Like I said," I tried to pull myself free once more and settled on taking a step away from him. "I have no idea. I'm not privy to how your precious Choosing ceremony works. Maybe you should take it up with Jayce." I tried to pull free again, but his grip tightened, and he closed the gap between us.

His nostrils flared and his jaw flexed. Warning bells went off in my head, telling me I needed to get away from him, now.

"Believe me, I will be," he said through gritted teeth. "Whatever the two of you are hiding, I will find out."

"I'm not hiding anything." I met his eyes as my abilities threatened to break through my control.

"I don't believe you." He grabbed me with his other hand. "I felt you push back on my illusion your first day here." Ice cold fear poured through me and settled in my stomach.

I opened my mouth to tell him he was crazy, but the look on my face must have given something away because he smiled. A black abyss fell around me, covering my surroundings in darkness. His arms released me and I spun around. Taking a few deep breaths, I tried to calm down and remember that this was just an illusion. He was trying to force me to use my abilities, to reveal myself, and I couldn't let that happen.

Aaron's laugh echoed around me as fear began to suffocate me. It was my worst nightmare. Any confinement bothered me, let alone this darkness that was consuming all my senses, trapping me in my own endless box. It felt like the walls – even if there were none - were closing in on me as I forced myself to take a step. And another. And another. With each breath, I felt like the air was getting thinner and thinner. What if I ran out of oxygen?

Chills ran down my skin as I tried to suck in another breath. My lungs were burning and my eyes started to tear up. I was going to suffocate. He was going to let me die. It seemed too real, and I'd never come up against an illusion this strong before. My heart rate began to speed up as I stumbled through the darkness, trying to find a way out of this nightmare. The pitch-black enveloped me with its cold embrace, and I cringed away from its icy touch. Everything and nothing folded into me, constricting my lungs until I was gasping with dizziness and had the urge to vomit. I held my head in my hands, trying to refocus my thoughts or do something to stop the madness from consuming me.

I didn't care about my ability's secrecy anymore. I *had* to get out. "Let me go," my voice quivered, and I hated how weak I sounded.

"Show me who you really are, then we can talk, Commoner."

"No," I whispered. Opening my eyes to the darkness I focused on my breathing. This wasn't real, there was plenty of air in the room. *Just breathe.*

"This is only your illusion." Deep breath. "Only an illusion," I repeated, louder and stronger this time. Anger took hold, replacing my fear and giving me enough adrenaline to focus on my abilities.

I remembered when I was younger and my brother and I would play hide and seek. We used our abilities to find each other- I could always sense his aura. I never thought that it would come in handy one day.

Scanning my surroundings, I noticed a red smoke-like string that connected me to Aaron. Just as I had practiced before as a child, I grabbed that string as hard as I could, and a few other pathways lit up, leading to the core of his illusion. Shooting through his mind, I found exactly what I was looking for. I grabbed the brightest red smoky line, yanked it from his grasp, and the darkness faded away.

"What's going on here?" Jayce's voice rang out loud and clear.

As the room came back into focus, Aaron's eyes locked on mine, and I challenged his stare. His icy blue eyes bore into me, and every part of my body was ready for him to attack. I shouldn't have been able to stop his illusions if I was just a Commoner, and now I'd done it twice.

"Nothing? Either of you?" Jayce stepped between us and looked back and forth.

Aaron composed himself and turned his attention to

his brother. "I was just informing the Commoner that she will not be excused from her tasks. If you require her help in the arena, it will have to be done after her work is complete each day." It was like he flipped a switch from murderous rage to a semi-nice big brother.

"You and I both know you can spare her from a few tasks." Jayce turned his back on me to face his brother.

"Not with the Gala coming up at the end of the month."

"Speaking of the Gala, that's why I'm here. I wanted to run a few things by you," Jayce let the topic of my to-do list complete*ly* fall to the wayside. *Gee, thanks.* I shook my head.

"A moment," he motioned Jayce toward the couch in the corner of the room. "There are a few items I need to wrap up with the servant."

Jayce nodded once and turned to me. "I'll expect you in the arena at the end of each day." Jayce's voice felt cool and detached and without another word, he stalked toward the couch.

Aaron closed the distance between us and guided me toward the elevator.

"This isn't over." He kept his voice low as he pressed the button on the wall. "I'll find out what's going on with you and when I do, you better pray to the Gods for mercy."

The elevator let out a sharp *ding* and the doors slid open.

"You do that, Scarlet," I said rushing onto the elevator and out of his grasp.

"I've sent you a new list of tasks to get done before the Gala. If even one item isn't up to standard, you can kiss any shred of freedom you have left goodbye."

The doors slid closed, but I could still feel his eyes boring into me as I started the descent. What the heck was I going to do? Both Aaron and Jayce were already too suspicious of me. I needed to get out of here, and maybe this Gala thing would be the perfect opportunity to slip away. I hated to admit it, but I needed to put my plans to find Eli on hold until I escaped the Starr residence. I needed to find out what this Gala was, and how I could use it to my advantage.

CHAPTER 14

The rest of the day went by in a blur. My mind was so consumed with escape, I paid little attention to the work I was doing. When the sun finally dipped below the horizon, I still had five things left to do on my list. Whatever this Gala was, it was taking a lot of work to prepare for, and I doubted I'd make it to the arena before Jayce went to sleep tonight. And honestly, I didn't care. The deal was that there would less work for me, and then I'd help him. He didn't hold up his end of the bargain, so who cared if I held up my end?

The next two things on my list involved curtains. I needed to bring up all the boxes from the basement to sort through and find fifty red curtains. Fifty! I had to read the number more than once, because who in their right mind had that many curtains? It seemed pointless to me to have to bring the boxes upstairs, then search through them. I had a sneaking suspicion Aaron was deliberately making this more tedious to punish me.

I made my way down to the basement. I was surprised to find that I actually had to manually turn on the overhead light on the stairs. Clearly, no Mystics ever came down here. The simple act of turning on a light would surely send them running for the hills.

The soft yellow light cast a warm glow on the stairs as I made my way into the belly of the house. As I reached the bottom of the staircase, I took in my surroundings. Boxes were stacked from floor to ceiling against every wall. I stared in horror. If Aaron thought I was going to haul all these boxes upstairs, he had another thing coming. It would take me days to get through them all, let alone haul them all upstairs.

"Hello, Willow," Alice's voice rang out and I nearly jumped out of my skin.

"You scared me half to death," I said clutching my chest.

"My apologies," she smiled. "Mr. Jayce wanted me to check on your progress."

"My progress." I rolled my eyes and a dry, humorless laugh escaped my throat. "How do you think it's going?" I waved my hand at all the unopened boxes. "I've barely had time to grab something to eat today and I still haven't finished Aaron's damn list." Anger and frustration coursed through my veins. "I'll be lucky to get some sleep before I have to start this nightmare over again tomorrow." I practically yelled at her.

Her pixel eyes stared at me, and her smile never left

her face. Immediately I felt bad. It wasn't her fault Aaron and Jayce were in a competition to drive me absolutely insane. She had been the only one to show me any sort of kindness since I arrived.

"I'm sorry," I took a deep breath and pinched the bridge of my nose. "Tell Jayce I won't be done for some time, and he shouldn't expect me in the arena this evening."

"Very well." Alice nodded and stepped toward me. "If there's anything I can help you with, don't hesitate to ask." She nodded once then disappeared.

At least I could cross Jayce off my list for today. Even though I'd rather be sitting on my ass torturing Jayce in the simulator, digging through all these boxes was the safer option. There was something about him that made me nervous, but not in the same way that Aaron did. And the fact that he may have gone out of his way to have me Chosen sent up all the red flags in my brain.

Stretching my neck and rolling my shoulders, I settled in for a long night of sifting through boxes. Starting with the right side of the room, I grabbed the stepstool and grabbed the first box. Setting it on the floor, I opened the box only to find old clothes. I pushed it to the side and went back up the ladder to pull down another box.

After my third stack of boxes, I finally found one with red curtains. They smelled musty and were covered in a layer of dust. It went without saying that I was going to have to get these cleaned. Pulling the fabric out of the box, I was surprised to find there were only two very long panels in the box. Carrying them upstairs I set them in a pile just outside the door to the basement.

"Two down, forty-eight to go."

I spent the next couple of hours going through boxes, pulling out curtains, and setting them aside. Finally, I turned to the last wall of boxes. I only needed one more curtain, and then I could move on with my life. I climbed up the step ladder and pulled the top box down. Immediately, I felt a stream of cool air brush across my face.

What the hell? I stared at the stone wall as if it had just cursed me out. Dropping the box I was holding to the ground, I pulled the next one from the stack, and the sweet scent of wet grass filled my nose. I tossed the box I was holding to the floor with the other one, pulled the next box off the stack, and froze.

The top of a stone arch stared back at me and I could feel the cool night air against my face. This must lead out of the house, but for what purpose? And what was a secret tunnel doing down here behind stacks of boxes? Did Aaron know it was here? Was he testing me or was he clueless about the arch?

The door at the top of the stairs creaked open and footsteps quickly followed. I placed the box back on the stack hiding the arch. If this was some secret forgotten passageway, it was probably best to leave it hidden. I jumped down from the stepstool and pried open one of the boxes on the floor, doing my best to look thoroughly engrossed in my work.

"Hope I'm not interrupting," Jayce said behind me.

I stood up to give him a piece of my mind, but my retort died on my lips.

Jayce stood in front of me with damp hair, a white t-shirt, and dark pants. My breath caught at the sight of him. I was used to seeing him either all dressed up or in his fighting gear looking stoic and unapproachable, but this was a different side to him, a casual side that radiated the same power but in a quiet understated way.

He was holding a plate of cakes, breads, and fruit.

"I was just grabbing something for my sweet tooth when I heard all the commotion down here." He gave me a tight-lipped smile. "Thought I'd check to see if everything was alright."

"Just peachy." I rolled my eyes and continued to pull a few items out of the box I was working on, in the hopes he would lose interest and leave.

"I was disappointed you weren't able to work the simulation this evening." He picked up a piece of fruit from his plate and popped it into his mouth.

"Yes, well if you'd held up your end of the bargain, we'd both be happier. Instead, I'm sorting through generations of your family's stuff." I held up an old dress and shook it at him.

"I told you I couldn't make any promises. Aaron is difficult at the best of times." He offered the plate of food to me and I grabbed one of the little tea cakes.

I snorted and rolled my eyes. "That's an understatement."

I popped the tea cake into my mouth and a tiny moan escaped my throat. I slapped a hand over my mouth, embarrassed. My cheeks flushed, and I wanted to go invisible right then and there, consequences be damned.

"You have good taste. Those are my favorite," he smirked. "Anne always makes a few extra for me."

"I'll admit, the food is one of the positive things about being here."

"One of the positives?" He cocked an eyebrow at me and a small smile formed on his lips.

"The only positive," I corrected. "With everything Aaron makes me do all day, the only joy I get to experience is when I'm eating."

"Speaking of Aaron, what happened between you two this morning?" He sat down on the stairs.

"Nothing." I pushed the box aside and started to open the other one I threw down.

"It didn't look like nothing." He cocked his head to the side and his eyes searched my face.

I shrugged. "Why do you even care? He's your brother and I'm just a Commoner here to serve you both."

"Because I know what it's like to be on the other end of his cruelty." My hands froze over the box and I looked up at him. His eyes met mine and my ability stirred inside me, sending a chill down my spine.

"Oh." It was the only word I could manage. His honesty took me completely off guard. "I'm sorry," I finally said, and I meant it. I couldn't imagine a world where my brother was my tormentor.

"There's no need to waste apologies on me." He shrugged and held the plate of food out toward me.

I pushed myself to my feet, and shoved the box aside to

close the distance between us. Plucking a grape from his plate, I popped it into my mouth.

"Besides, I made you a promise that no one would hurt you here." The corner of his lips twitched into a shy grin, but it didn't reach his eyes.

There was a part of me that wanted to tell him Aaron had forced another illusion on me, but the rest of me knew to keep quiet. This could be a setup to see if I would break my silence about Aaron. Jayce seemed different, like he might actually care, but the truth was, I didn't know him and the only person I trusted right now was myself.

I shrugged. "Nothing happened," I lied, and out of the corner of my eye I saw his shoulders slump. It's like he knew I was lying, but he didn't seem relieved about it. "He just asked me a few questions," I added.

"Oh? What about?" He looked up at me.

"About how I was Chosen."

"Best in your class? All the volunteering and community work, or maybe it was your impeccable desire to serve Mystics?" The corner of his eyes crinkled as he smiled.

I snorted out a laugh. "Yeah, well, I definitely didn't do any of that," I said folding my arms across my chest. "Which is why your brother is very curious about how I was Chosen. He thinks you had something to do with it." I watched him carefully for any sign that what I was saying might be true.

"Why would I have something to do with you being Chosen?" He furrowed his brow and leaned forward ever so slightly.

"Because you were there the day of the ceremony."

He picked up a piece of fruit and rolled it between his fingers before tossing it into his mouth.

"I've been to plenty of Choosing ceremonies in the past. We both have. So that can't be it."

I debated if I should keep my mouth shut or not. As much as I didn't want to get in trouble for being a snitch, I also wanted answers of my own.

"He said you hand-picked me, though." I held his gaze, and he didn't look away from me. Nor did he say anything. "That your interest in me is out of character." I forced the words out and felt my cheeks flush.

He shook his head and his eyes fell from mine. The sharp stab of embarrassment and anger shot through me like a hot knife.

"So, it's true?" I took a step back from him. Every nerve in my body screamed. If he had hand-picked me to come here, then that meant he had a plan for me. Whatever it was, I wanted no part in it.

He stood and my abilities burned at the surface of my skin. I was afraid that if he took one step in my direction, I would let them take over.

"What purpose would I have for Choosing you?" He lifted his eyes so that he was staring down at me and the warmth and softness that was there a moment ago was gone. "You don't want to be here, and you said it yourself, you don't exactly qualify as outstanding."

His words felt like a punch to the gut, and I hated that he had any effect on me. Sure, I didn't want to be a part of some nefarious plan, but it still hurt that yet another person saw me as nothing.

"Glad we cleared that up," I said through gritted teeth. "And if you're done insulting me, I'd like to get back to work." I turned my back on him and grabbed at the box without waiting for a response.

A few seconds went by and then I heard him walk up the stairs, and the door closed behind him. Frustrating, anger, and hurt bubbled to the surface and I pulled the last out of the box.

I'll show him outstanding.

CHAPTER 15

The early morning light was just beginning to creep into my bedroom when a series of *pings!* rang out from my tablet. Gods, would they ever leave me alone? I rolled over, trying to get back to sleep, but the table kept ringing, and I began to worry that something bad had happened. Muttering to myself, I grabbed it and I let my eyes focus on the screen.

Penthouse. Now- Aaron. Good morning to you too, jerk.

A rare message from Jayce followed: *Shower and dress nicely before you get up here.* I didn't like the sound of that. What reason would there possibly be to look presentable at this hour?

Don't keep me waiting. Aaron again. A little torn on who to listen to, I decided to meet them halfway. I went to the bathroom and washed up, braiding my hair neatly instead of my go-to messy bun. Then, I put on a tight, knee-length skirt with a flowy top, and tried to rinse some of the dust off my shoes. Everything I owned now smelled faintly of floor polish, and I made a mental note to ask Alice for some help with that. There must be a way around the stench, or I'd start to smell it in my dreams. I glanced quickly in the mirror before heading out the door and catching the elevator up to the penthouse, getting ready for whatever storm was about to hit me.

A million different scenarios ran through my head. Did they check the search history on my tablet? Did someone see me leave the house to head into town and rat me out? Did *Jayce* rat me out? Had Eli come to save me from this humiliating existence? None of the scenarios in my head ended well. Aaron would never let me serve another household, whether it was my brother or not.

The elevator doors opened and I stepped into the room, bracing myself for whatever was coming. Aaron and Jayce were there, as well as Alice who gave me her usual wide smile. Sitting in the chair that Aaron usually sat in was a man I had never met before, but recognized from his portraits around the house: Cain Starr.

"How nice of you to grace us with your presence, Ms. Knight." Aaron's tone was even more sharp than usual. Jayce gave a subtle shake of his head, warning me to not test his brother today as I opened my mouth to respond. I didn't need the advice. I couldn't risk Aaron throwing me into one of his illusions with his father around. The moment I stepped foot in the penthouse and saw who had arrived, I felt my powers start to build up beneath my skin, and I was worried about losing control. If he saw me pull out of Aaron's illusion, he would never give up until he figured out how I did it. I tried my best for an apologetic tone.

"Apologies, Sir." *Keep your mouth shut, Willow. The only words you now know are 'yes, sir' and 'no, sir'.*

Aaron's eyebrows raised almost all the way to his hairline, obviously not used to me behaving myself. Behind him I could see Jayce raise his eyebrows as well. "As I'm sure even a Commoner could notice, my father, the ruler of the Scarlets, has come for a visit."

Should I curtsy? I wasn't really prepared to meet royalty today.

"It's an honor, sir," I said, keeping my eyes on the floor. He didn't bother to respond. Aaron was fuming. I had a feeling he was hoping I'd be my usual combative self so he had an excuse to show his father how forceful he could be with the servants when they stepped out of line. Well, if he wanted to make an example out of someone, it sure as heck wasn't going to be me. Could he punish me for behaving myself after his parents left? Maybe. But disrespecting a Starr in the presence of their patriarch would have much more serious consequences, so I had to pick my battles.

"My parents will be here for a few days to conduct some business in the region. While they are here you are to follow their instructions to the best of your...*limited* abilities. Their requests come first, even above mine." He didn't have to mention that whatever Jayce needed from me would come last. He seemed almost excited that he could keep me from helping his brother with whatever we might be doing in the stimulator. I didn't have the nerve to tell him that he was doing me a favor too. The more time I spent with Jayce the harder it was to keep up with the lie that I was just a Commoner. Plus, what if Mr. Starr decided to come and check out what his son was doing late at night all alone with a Commoner? Would I be able to say no if he asked me to demonstrate what Jayce was studying with me? Would I be able to fake it if I was forced into that stimulator in his presence? I wasn't sure.

"Yes, Mr. Starr," I answered, still trying my best to sound respectful. Cain Starr had yet to glance up in my direction, his eyes fixed on his sons, his mouth set in a hard line. I wondered what kind of business had brought him back here. From what I had learned from the other servants and conversations I had overheard around town, Cain Starr was eager to retire to the countryside and let his son take over as Scarlet leader. He had left the house to travel as a trial run for Aaron, to test his leadership ability and make sure he was ready without officially stepping away. Apparently Aaron contacted his father almost every day to talk to him about how it was all going. Maybe Mr. Starr wasn't happy with his son's performance.

"Ms. Knight," Jayce began, and I whipped my head around to face him, "We will be having a formal dinner in the dining hall tonight. You will help serve. Please follow Alice back to your room for instructions on the proper way to do so. We wouldn't want any mishaps. It would reflect poorly on my brother and I. Remember, they might be our parents, but first and foremost they are the leaders of the Scarlets."

I couldn't tell if it was a plea to keep me in line for his

sake, or a warning to not mess up for my own sake. Either way, he got his point across. I would be a perfect Commoner servant. Heck, I'd even ask Alice to teach me how to curtsy properly.

"Yes, Sir," I said, bowing my way out of the room and feeling absolutely ridiculous. How much of an idiot did they think I was that I couldn't handle dinner? It wasn't like they expected me to cook it, too.

"Ms. Knight, come with me, please!" Alice said. Did she always have to sound do cheery? It drove me crazy.

A few minutes and an elevator ride later, we were back in my room, where Alice was rummaging through my drawers picking out my outfit for later. Honestly, better her than me. Everything she pulled out she folded neatly and set aside in a nice pile. I would have probably just thrown it around the room until I found what I was looking for. Finally, she stood up with an outfit in her hand- slim black pants and a white button-down top that had cuffed sleeves.

"All the servants have an outfit like this. Mrs. Starr likes things to be uniform!" Alice explained. *I bet she does,* I thought.

"So, when you enter the dining room- promptly at 6 o'clock please!- you will stand towards the front of the room until it's time to serve the wine," Alice began. "Do you want to write this down, dear? Ok. One of the other servants will hand you the wine when it's time to start pouring. Start with Mrs. Starr, then Mr. Starr, and then Aaron and Jayce. Age order for the sons, don't forget! It would be a great insult, especially for the heir to the Scarlets, to be served after his younger brother."

Gods, I wish I could serve Jayce first just to see Aaron's reaction, but I knew when to pick my battles. Alice droned on for another hour about proper protocol for serving meals, and I wrote everything down to study as I did my other chores for the day. I might hate serving Mystics, but I knew better than to try my luck with the Starr family in this situation.

I was nervous, no matter how detailed Alice's instructions were. In school, we had etiquette lessons designed to prepare us for these situations. Designed *only* for these situations. But since I never expected to be chosen, I never bothered to pay attention in those classes. Or even show up most of the time. Gods, I was so dumb. If my teachers could see me now, they would be laughing in my face. How many of them had answered *'you never know!'* when I told them I'd never need to remember any of this stuff? And now look at me, cowering in my polished shoes and clean shirt over a simple dinner. Three courses. How long could that take? I just had to get through a couple of hours of lingering in the shadows until someone's glass was empty, and pray I didn't spill anything.

I spent the rest of the day memorizing my notes as best as I could while completing the tasks assigned to me, but it wasn't easy. My to-do list was at least twice as long as usual, with the added two residents assigning chores from weeding the garden around their favorite benches to steaming their shirts and dresses and polishing their shoes. The only good thing about the day was that I successfully avoided all members of the Starr family. And thank the Gods, because my nerves were frazzled and I felt like any little thing might allow my powers to break free. My breathing exercises did nothing, and my skin was crawling by the time I got back to my room to shower before dinner.

Standing under the water I kept repeating to myself every note I could remember from Alice's lecture. *Serve from the right side, serve women first, then head of household, then by age, fill the water glasses an inch from the top, turn the wine bottle as your pulling away to avoid spilling, don't look any of them in the eye....*

It was enough to make anyone's head spin, and I let myself go invisible in the shower just to let out some of the pressure building behind my eyes as I desperately tried to stay calm. I hadn't been able to eat anything all day, mostly because I was so nervous, but also because I had so little time to myself for more than a few quite bites of bread I managed to grab from the kitchens. I had a feeling Aaron had purposely targeted me for every extra task his parents needed instead of spreading it around to the other servants. Gods, I hated him. I hated all the Mystics, even Jayce right now, whose shirt I had to steam so he could be presentable for dinner.

I braided my hair and let it fall down my back, praying the unruly strands would stay put for one evening, got into my uniform for the night, and headed down to the dining hall with a few minutes to spare.

CHAPTER 16

Mystics were ridiculous. Everything I learned about them just made me realize it more and more. I walked into the dining room, exactly on time and looking presentable, and barely contained my snort when I saw what greeted me.

Aaron and Jayce were dressed in suits, tailored to perfection and pressed beautifully. Their hair was combed, their nails cleaned. They were sitting straight-backed, quietly, with a humble look on their faces, hands folded neatly in front of them. They had taken seats across from each other in the middle of the enormous dining table. At the heads of the table sat Mr. Starr and his wife.

How are they even going to speak to each other sitting this far away? I asked myself, trying hard not to giggle at the idea of them screaming over their dinner plates. I had always known Mystics had a flair for the dramatic, but this just might win for most unbelievable display of stupidity I had ever seen. I couldn't take my eyes off the scene, and a nudge at my side startled me as Michael, one of the other servants, handed me a bottle of wine and nodded towards the table.

I walked towards the table and started with Jayce's mom Eleanor, as Alice had instructed me earlier. Avoiding eye contact with her, I poured a glass of wine, careful not to spill a drop onto the pristine white tablecloth. I breathed a small sigh of relief when I was successful, and allowed myself to study her. She looked like Aaron, tall and blonde, with hard blue eyes. She sat perfectly, so straight it looked uncomfortable. Mrs. Starr didn't look like a woman who smiled often. Her dress was neat and tidy, and her hair was perfectly in place, not a strand escaping the tight bun pulled to the nape of her neck.

I thought of my mom, her easy smile and laugh, and felt sorry for Jayce. I had judged him for having the perfect life, the perfect family. But I couldn't imagine his mom playing with him, getting muddy in the rain, holding his hand while he cried. She was so....cold. It was obvious she tolerated absolutely zero nonsense. Jayce and Aaron's childhood was probably not a fun one.

Making my way to the other side of the table, legs shaking only a little bit, I poured Mr. Starr's wine.

"Thank you," he said as I finished. "You must be the newest servant. We didn't get a chance to speak earlier. How are you finding your new home?"

Friendly, but I could tell by his cruel eyes that he didn't really care. Was pretending he hadn't completely ignored me earlier for some kind of power play? Or was he just performing for his wife and the rest of the household in the room? Cain Starr had darker hair than his wife and sons, but the same icy stare. I made sure to keep my eyes on the ground as I answered him.

"Very good, sir, thank you." He wasn't getting anything from me. I knew my place tonight.

"Hm. That will be all." I felt my body release a tension I didn't know it was holding as he dismissed me. Although Aaron had taken over the running of the household, his father was still the leader of the Scarlets. He was basically a king, and it was hard to not be afraid when I was standing in his presence. He was the leader for a reason, and I was worried he would take one look at me and instantly know I was hiding something big. I could *feel* my blood, my *silver* blood, pumping through my body, and although it was impossible, I worried that Cain Starr could see it moving inside me.

I moved around the table to pour wine for Jayce, my steps wobbling just a little, but he raised his eyebrows and gave me a slight, wide-eyed look. *Damn*, I owed him big time. Alice told me to do it in age order, and if I have poured for Jayce first, Aaron would have made my life hell. That is, if his parents didn't get to me first. I took a shaky breath in, and moved to Aaron's side of the table to pour his glass. I could feel his eyes on me every step of the way, and I knew if I looked at him, I would see the hatred written all over his face. This was going to be a long dinner.

When Jayce's wine was finally served, the kitchen servants brought in the soup. At first, the only sound in the room was the clinking of silverware, and I thought I would explode from the awkward tension of it all. Finally, Mr. Starr spoke.

"Aaron, how is the preparation for the Gala going?"

"Well, Father," Aaron answered, "Although it's hard to find good help nowadays, I have some exciting things planned, and the preparations are going very nicely."

"I've heard about these 'exciting things', Aaron, and one of the reasons I came here was to put a stop to it."

Uh-oh. I backed away, closer to the wall, wishing I could turn invisible.

"Father, will all due respect-"

"Respect? You want to talk to me about respect? I have dedicated my life, my service to the Scarlets, my legacy, to erasing the barbaric practices of the past, and I learn through whispers and rumors that my heir is preparing to tear all of that down before he even steps fully into my position!"

"Father, if I'm to be taken seriously as your heir, I need to make a name for myself."

"The Starr name isn't enough, Aaron?" Mr. Starr's tone could have frozen the sun. I held my breath, waiting for a response. Gods, it was amazing to watch the bastard squirm.

"The Starr name is more than enough, Father," Aaron started, sounding hesitant. "But you and mother are well-respected for your wisdom and fairness, and my brother's abilities are considered the strongest among all of us. I get left behind, forgotten, and I have something to prove before I can take my place as ruler."

"What do you care – " Mr. Starr began angrily, but another voice cut him off.

"Darling," Mrs. Starr interrupted, her tone warm, but leaving no room for further discussion. "Perhaps this is a conversation for another time?" Her eyes glanced around the room to me and the other servants. *Never let them see the cracks,* I thought. As different as she was from my mother, I saw a little bit of myself in her. I had to admit, I kind of liked her. Three strong men in the room, and she was clearly in charge.

With a soft cough, the other servants startled me out of my focus on the conversation. Time to clean up the soup bowls. I took Mrs. Starr and Jayce's dish, and let someone else grab Aaron's. I wouldn't put it past him to trip me as I walked past him. His face was red, and I could see his hands shaking slightly.

"Jayce, darling," Mrs. Starr asked as we placed the main course in front of her, "How is your friend Jaxtyn?"

Small talk. No wonder Eleanor Starr was considered one of the most skilled noblewomen in the world. She shifted the conversation with ease into safe territory. As the family slipped into casual conversation, I felt my mind wandering. I didn't really care about their lives, and I knew Jayce wasn't going to talk about his secret alleyway visits, so there was nothing for me to learn here that I didn't already know.

The rest of the meal passed uneventfully, none of the men willing to disobey Mrs. Starr and slip back into the argument that was still bubbling right under the surface. It was endearing, really, seeing them like this. They were a family- a regular, flawed family. It would almost be cute, if they weren't monsters. These were the people who took my mother away from me. It was their fault I would never have a family dinner like this again. I couldn't let myself forget that. It was too dangerous.

Later that evening, I was sitting in my bed after a shower, sighing as I put my feet up. Today had been stressful. I was glad the Starr parents were only stopping in for a few days. They were terrifying, and with my birthday approaching my powers were getting harder and harder to control. What was going to happen when I reached my birthday? Would I explode? I really didn't know much about what happened when a Mystic hit twenty years old. We always just learned that Mystics 'came into their full power' at that point, whatever that meant. I was barely keeping it together now, so the thought of my powers getting even stronger was terrifying. Should I find somewhere to hide that day, just in case?

I was trying to figure out the best way to avoid the entire family for the next few days to keep myself calm when a knock at the door startled me. *What is it now?* I asked myself. *Prince Aaron needs his pillows fluffed?* I considered ignoring it and pretending I was asleep, but I wouldn't put it past them to insist that someone break down my door and rip me from my bed if I didn't see what they wanted, so I got up and walked to the door without getting properly dressed, not caring if Alice or one of the other servants saw me in my pajamas. When I opened the door, a pair of blue eyes met mine, and I almost gasped out loud.

"I'm sorry to interrupt your evening," Jayce said, looking a little sheepish, and holding something behind his back. I stood there for a few seconds, long enough for it to be awkward, before answering.

"You're not interrupting anything. I was just resting. Would you...like to come in?" I asked, not sure if that was an appropriate question.

I had never seen either Starr brother on this floor. The servant's quarters were beneath their dignity, and if they wanted us they would either send a message, or have Alice come fetch us. Jayce looked out of place, and more than a little uncomfortable.

"Ah, no. Thank you," he said. "I just came to give you this." He pulled his hands from behind his back. He held up a basket with the most delicious smell coming out of it. My mouth watered instantly, and I had to fight not to drool on Jayce's expensive shoes.

"What is this?"

"Your stomach rumbled out loud throughout the entire meal. I'm shocked no one said anything."

I blushed. I thought I had gotten away with that since no one said anything, but maybe the Starr's were too proper to point out their starving servant and her loud stomach.

"You should stop skipping meals, you know. I had the chefs pack the leftovers from tonight into the basket for you," Jayce said. If it wasn't his and his brother's fault that

I was missing meals, I would have been touched. *Don't fall for his charm, Willow.*

"I didn't have time –" I started, angrily. Jayce cut me off.

"Ms. Knight, just say thank you and take the food. I can't stand here all night. My mother would disown me if she knew I was standing here in your doorway."

The ridiculousness, and danger, of the situation dawned on me- the little boy sneaking off to see his wrong-side-of-the-tracks friend. Friend, or charity case. I never really knew where I stood with Jayce, since his moods changed like the wind, but right now he was being kind. And stupid. The Starr's would never allow such an embarrassment. Jayce would be scolded, punished even. I would be sent away, maybe even killed, if they knew he was standing here.

Some of my anger faded away. This was a nice gesture, no matter how misguided it might be. Maybe Jayce wasn't used to having many friends. Maybe he didn't realize the target he was putting on my back, or thought he could protect me from harm. But he was right, the longer he stood here, the more dangerous it became.

"Thank you," I said, taking the basket from his hand. "Good night."

"Sweet dreams, Ms. Knight. Try and stay out of trouble."

I shut the door in his face, and hated the smile that spread across mine as I greedily dove into the basket of food.

CHAPTER 17

I'd finally gotten the hang of things over the last week, and my list of tasks had gotten easier to manage now that the Starr parents had left and I was more familiar with the residence. I hadn't been alone with Jayce since he brought me food a week ago, and Alice never came back to request I join him in the simulation again. I guess helping with the simulation wasn't that important after all. Or possibly he was avoiding me until his parents left. And I might have been doing the same. I didn't want to get on the bad side of Cain and Eleanor Starr.

I couldn't help being suspicious of him, no matter how nice he was to me sometimes. If he hadn't hand-picked me to serve his family, then he'd have no reason to get defensive or vanish completely once I called him out on it. Maybe Aaron was right after all. The thought made my skin crawl and a knot formed in the pit of my stomach.

I had woken before the sun this morning. I crawled out of bed and made my way in the dark to the bathroom to splash some water on my face. The automatic lights switched on as soon as I stepped into the bathroom, and as I looked up into the mirror, I was startled by what I saw. I looked the same, but barely recognized myself. The spark behind my eyes had all but disappeared and was replaced by dark circles. My skin felt too tight as my abilities rolled beneath the surface, pushing to break free. I shuddered at the thought of coming into my full power in just a few short weeks. There'd be no way to hide who or what I was once I turned twenty.

My chest tightened as I tried to take a deep breath to calm myself. I came here with a plan: Ruin the Mystics' perfect little bubble and find my brother. But everything had gone to crap so quickly. I took another deep breath, but it did little to calm my nerves. I'd been stuck inside for far too long. I needed to feel the sun on my face, taste the fresh air, feel the thrill of other people moving around me as if I was nothing more than a shadow.

Without making the conscious decision to sneak out again, I was back in my room and changed into the Mystic clothes I used before to blend in. There were still a few book stores I needed to check out on my list, and today seemed like just as good a day as any. My search had stalled when Cain and Eleanor Starr came to visit. It was much too risky sneaking out with them around.

I let my abilities take hold and slipped into my invisibility in record time. Already I felt lighter as I let my true nature take control. Sneaking out was much easier now that I knew the property better, and I let myself out a side door off the kitchen.

The air was much cooler than I anticipated, and I was grateful for the warmer clothing. Taking a deep breath of fresh air, again I felt a small part of me click into place. Before coming here, I'd spent most of my life outside. Being stuck inside all the time was literally sucking the life from me. How people managed to spend their days indoors and not lose their minds was a mystery to me.

I made my way around the house and down the steep driveway in a matter of minutes. As my feet hit the main street, the tension from the last week started to melt away. I looked up at the light blue sky through the canopy of trees and sighed. Most of the leaves had changed to a bright red and orange, leaving very few leaves untouched by the change in seasons.

All was quiet on the street except for the happy chirping of birds, and I couldn't help but smile. Despite everything that's happened over the last couple of weeks, nothing could take away the simple joy of dawn. No matter my troubles, the birds would always sing their songs as the sun rose, and I took a small comfort in that.

Slipping into the same bushes I had the last time I snuck out, I reigned in my invisibility and became solid once more. It might have been safer to stay invisible, but if I found Eli, it'd be impossible to reappear out of nowhere in the middle of town. It was a risk going into town dressed as a Mystic, but it was even risker to out myself as something other.

I started toward the bookshop closest to the Starr

house. It was only a few blocks away, so I'd have plenty of time to look for my brother and get back without anyone noticing. I'd debated on which bookshop I should check out next, but I figured I should just go in order of location since my first guess was a complete bust. At least when it came to Eli. Jayce on the other hand-

I shook my head and pushed Jayce from my mind. I hated to admit it, but he had become a constant nag on my thoughts since that night in the basement. I couldn't figure him out, what motivated him, why he was nice to me one minute and cold the next. He was impossible to nail down. I'd never had this much trouble sorting someone out before. On the whole, people were fairly easy to read, but Jayce... Jayce was different. I let out a breath and shook my head. Right now was not the time to be distracted by Jayce, his plans for me, what he hiding, or where he disappeared to.

I turned right at the corner and was surprised to see a handful of people already milling about. I kept my head down as I moved past a group of girls my age who were engrossed in a story one of them was telling about the gown she was going to wear to the Gala. It seemed everyone was excited for the extravagant party the Starr family was hosting. I didn't get it. It was just a party, but everyone was acting like the Gods themselves would be in attendance.

I turned left down the next street and almost knocked into a woman and her daughter. Everyone seemed to be out this morning, moving from shop to shop, trying to get the first pick of cakes, teas, meat, and drinks. If I didn't think too much about where I was, I could almost pretend I was back home. A thrill ran through me, and my fingers twitched with anticipation. The crowded street and busy customers were the perfect opportunity for me to add to my collection of coins and trinkets.

I could see the bookshop up ahead just starting to open its doors and wheel out carts of books, so I decided I could spare a few minutes to search for a worthy target. I stopped in front of one of the shops, pretending to be interested in the display while I searched the reflection for someone who wasn't paying enough attention to their surroundings.

Within seconds, I noticed a woman wistfully walking through the crowd. She stopped and looked at each shop with disinterest and then moved along the path, bumping into people as she carried on. It was clear her mind was elsewhere, which meant she'd be the perfect target.

I stepped away from the window and followed the woman down the street, waiting for her to stop again so I could make my move.

When she came to a halt in front of a bakery, I came up behind her, and without skipping a beat, knocked right into her. In one swift movement, I was able to unclasp the watch from her wrist and shove it into the pocket of my dress. A surge of adrenaline ran through me as I apologized and quickly moved past her. I'd never enjoyed stealing from the Commoners back in the village, since they didn't have much to spare. But stealing from a Mystic? Sign me up.

Boney fingers wrapped around my wrist and pulled

me backward. "Clearly you've never tried stealing from an aura-reader before," the woman's voice was calm and soft. She spun me around and stared down at me. And I was surprised to see that she wasn't angry.

She was about my height, maybe a little taller, with gorgeous, silky golden hair. Her deep-set, warm, coffee-brown eyes fringed with dark, sweeping eyelashes made me think of a princess. For all I knew, she could be one. Her clear, milky skin looked smooth to touch.

Ice cold panic poured through me, and my heart felt like it was in my stomach. I hadn't been caught since I was a kid, when it was easy to play the innocent hungry child. I couldn't use that excuse now- I was all dressed up as one of them.

"Interesting," she murmured with a small smile. "Who are you?"

I had no words for her. It felt like a trap. No one was this nice to someone who just got caught trying to steal from them.

"Go on then, unless you want me to call for the authorities."

"No," I practically yelled. "Please."

"Your name then, girl." It was a demand, but still, she seemed more curious than angry.

"Willow," I responded crisply, not wanting to give anything more away.

"I'm Lilliana, a healer from the Gold region." She let go of her grip on my wrist and extended her hand for me to shake.

"Erm, hi." I shook her hand hesitantly and her eyes lit up.

"What region are you from?" Her eyes danced across my face as she reached out with her other hand and placed it on top of our joined hands.

"I'm a Commoner." I met her gaze, refusing to back down or be seen as weak.

"Really?" Her brow furrowed as she looked at me. "That can't be right. I'm the strongest aura reader alive. My senses are never wrong." Her grip tightened and she pulled me closer to her.

Shoot. I had to go and pick the one person who could sense there was something more to me than meets the eyes. If I truly was a Commoner, she shouldn't be able to sense a magical aura from me. This was bad. Like, really bad.

"Your aura is lilac? It doesn't match any Mystic's I've seen before. I almost didn't notice you, honestly. It's dull, barely there just around the edges." Her eyes moved around me as she looked at the invisible aura surrounding me. "Why are you hiding yourself, Willow?"

"I'm not hiding anything," I lied. I didn't know how to suppress my aura. I never had training with that, as much as I would have liked to.

"I don't believe you." Her pink lips tilted up into a small smile. "And I think the authorities might be interested in a thief with an aura of someone who doesn't belong."

"No, please don't. It would mean death for me."

She paused and looked me up and down, taking in the

clothes I was wearing. It was as if she was really seeing me for the first time. I thanked the Gods I'd chosen an outfit that was understated for a Mystic. At least she couldn't say for sure that I was trying to fake being a Mystic.

"Are you a servant?"

I nodded and pulled my hand from her grasp. She didn't fight me and I felt a sense of relief wash over me. I was pretty sure I could outrun her if it came to that.

"You're afraid of what they will do to you if they find out about your little indiscretion." It wasn't a question. She could see it all over my face that I was terrified of Aaron finding out. An image of him popped into my head and dread filled the pit of my stomach. He would be elated for a reason to punish me. My abilities sizzled across my skin, and I had to fight to keep them under control.

Her expression softened and she held out her hand for the watch. "Everyone deserves a second chance."

I dropped the watch into her open palm and braced myself to make a run for it.

"You're better than this." She placed a hand on my shoulder like she knew I wanted to bolt.

"You don't know that," I said under my breath.

"Ahh, but I do. I can see the essence of who you are, and you're a good person." She looked at me like a mother disappointed in her child.

I opened my mouth to thank her for her kindness when a familiar voice called my name, and I froze.

CHAPTER 18

"Willow! Willow, is that you? Oh my Gods!" There he was, my big brother. I hadn't seen him in eleven years, but he still had that same easy smile and kind eyes. He was taller now, and when he smiled there were some lines around his eyes, but he was still the same Eli. *My* Eli.

"Eli!" I grinned as I leaped into his open arms. He squeezed me tight and spun me in a circle before putting me back on my feet and holding me at arm's length. It was like a dream.

"What are you doing here?" His eyes searched my face and his worried his brow as he looked down at me. "Is everything alright at home?"

"I wouldn't know," I shrugged, trying my best to sound grown up and as brave as he had always told me to be. "I was Chosen a few weeks ago," I said, watching his expression change from worry to amusement. He looked like he wanted to laugh at the absurdity that *I* could ever be Chosen. Even as a child, I had been a handful. He smiled and shook his head. "There must have been some mistake."

"That was my reaction too," I admitted sheepishly. "But nope, I'm here, for real."

"Wow, just wow." He let out a belly laugh, and I couldn't help but smile.

"Tell me about it."

"I don't mean to interrupt this little reunion," Lilliana looked to Eli. "But how do you know this girl, Eli?" Lilliana looked between the two of us unable to see how Eli with his dark hair, sharp edges, and Mystic blood could possibly know me, a skinny Commoner thief.

"She's my sister, Willow! The one I told you about." Eli pulled me against him and smiled. "Don't you see the resemblance?" he joked, and we both laughed. We stopped looking anything alike by the time I was five.

"Of course she is," she smirked as she looked between the two of us.

"What's that supposed to mean?" He looked down at me and back up at Lilliana.

My perfect reunion was going to be ruined once Eli found out I'd tried stealing from her.

My eyes met Lilliana's and she shook her head a fraction of an inch and smiled. I nodded once, in silent agreement to just drop the whole stealing thing.

"Your auras have a similar feel to them."

Eli beamed completely unaware of the silent conversation between Lilliana and me.

Thank you, I mouthed, and she nodded once.

"So, you two know each other?" I bit my bottom lip and motioned between the two of them.

"We've been friends for a few years. She comes to this region quite often," Eli looked up at Lilliana and something silent passed between them as well. This woman was a keeper of many secrets, it seemed. A silence fell between us for a few seconds as I watched Lilliana and Eli curiously, wondering what secret she was keeping for him.

"So, how've you been enjoying the Scarlet region?" Eli let go of me and folded his arms across his chest.

"It's ahh...different," I rubbed the back of my neck. I really didn't want to have this conversation in front of a stranger.

"What's wrong?" He furrowed his brow and took a step toward me.

"Do you think we could talk in private?" I murmured and smiled awkwardly towards Lilliana.

"You can trust her, she already knows everything. Lilli has been the one person outside of you I've been able to trust," he said sheepishly.

"Everything?" I asked under my breath.

"You know what I mean, you don't have to worry about her. Being an aura reader, she knows things even if I chose not to share them with her."

Analyzing Lilliana again, I wasn't sure. Someone who was willing to keep secrets for nothing in return always had an angle. She seemed like a nice enough person, but my distrust of the world went deep, and one kind gesture wasn't going to change that. Plus, I hadn't seen my brother in so long. I wanted to be alone with him, to try and get to know him again, and learn about the person he'd become.

"Please Eli?" I held his eyes, willing him to understand that I needed my brother.

"I'll meet you at the bookshop." Lilliana leaned close to Eli and placed her hand on his chest.

"Lilli, you don't-"

She waved him off. "It's not every day you're reunited with your sister."

Eli nodded. "I'll see you in a bit."

Lilliana turned to me and gave me a tight-lipped smile. "It was nice meeting you, Willow. I do hope we cross paths again some time."

"Nice meeting you as well."

And with that, she continued down the street. She still wore the same sort of bemused expression, but now I recognized it for what it was. She was reading auras.

"Of all the regions you could've been placed in, you end up here. I still can't believe it's really you. Who are you serving?" Eli wrapped an arm around my shoulders and walked me towards a bench.

"Aaron and Jayce Starr."

It was as if I slapped the smile off his face. He stopped in his tracks and looked at me. "You're joking."

I shook my head and was glad he understood how screwed I was.

"That's,,, well…not great," Eli groaned. "I mean, any other house would have better."

"Why do you say that?"

"Aaron will be the leader of the Scarlet Region once his father officially steps down, and his brother Jayce," he ran a hand through his hair. "Well, people say he's the most powerful Mystic out there, Will."

"He's not so scary once you get to know him. At least, not so scary all the time."

He shook his head and gestured for me to sit down, and then took the seat next to me. . "The stories people tell, it's hard to believe they're true sometimes. I wouldn't believe them if I hadn't seen what he was capable of with my own eyes." He shook his head as if he was recalling some memory or Jayce.

"Eli, tell me. What did you see him do?"

"Have they explained how policing works here? Who gets punished and how?"

A chill ran through me. I hadn't even really considered it, but if the Starr family were the leaders of the Scarlets…

"Aaron and Jayce decide, Willow. And since Aaron is the leader, he gets to choose the punishment, and Jayce has to dole it out."

"Eli, you're not saying…"

"The Starr family would have been the ones to allow the killing of our mom the night they came to get me."

My world flipped over, and I couldn't breathe. No. *No.*

"Jayce would have been young, probably around your age, no more. I think they had a birthday celebration for him a few years back when he turned twenty. He didn't have any input in the decision. And neither did Aaron, I guess. But it was still their parents."

I nodded, not trusting myself to speak.

I thought about how often Jayce trained in the arena. The way he moved in the simulations and how he always seemed to be pushing himself. I'd never really considered the reason for it, since Lapis were known as the more brutish Mystics, and I didn't really think Scarlets had any reason to fight when they could just use their illusions.

"And now? Does Jayce make the decisions and perform the punishments himself?"

"Yes, he does. He insists on doing it himself. He says that if he and his brother are making the decisions on how to punish people who break the law, then they should have the courage to dole out those punishments themselves as well. It's certainly made them less severe in their punishments, but they still hurt people who break the rules. And it's not like he needs any help from a Lapis to do it. He's the most powerful Mystic there is."

"If he's so powerful, then why isn't he the leader?" I couldn't help wanting to know more about Jayce and his family now that I had seen them in action, and add another piece to the puzzle. Maybe an outsider's opinion would shed some light on the mystery that was Jayce Starr.

"He's not the elder brother," he shrugged. "He's involved in leadership decisions, but he's not the boss. And he probably never will be, but I think he likes it that way. Jayce doesn't really socialize much, so no one really knows what his story is. Honestly, he seems kind of like a dick to me."

A twinge of discomfort pulled at my chest. I wasn't

Jayce's number one fan or anything, but something about the disdain in Eli's voice made me uncomfortable.

"What?" Eli eyed me.

"I don't know, Jayce seems okay." I bit the inside of my cheek. "Aaron's the real dick."

"Lower your voice," Eli looked around as if someone was going to jump out and haul me off to be punished. "You can't say things like that."

"You just did about Jayce," I argued.

"Yeah, well, he's not the one in charge."

"Whatever," I rolled my eyes. "Speaking from experience, Jayce isn't that bad. He's secretive and I can never tell what his motives are, but at least he treats me like a person."

"Will," Eli shook his head. "You need to be careful with him. Remember that it was his family who decided that one of our parents should die for my indiscretion."

"As if I'm anything but?" I rolled my eyes. I was glad that I hadn't known this before I served the Starr parents, because they certainly gave the order to have my family destroyed. But Jayce and Aaron…I wasn't sure they were as brutal as their father. Especially not Jayce. And it wasn't like I could hate Mystics any more than I already did. I knew now that I had to keep a closer eye on them now, though.

"I'm serious. They can't find out about..." he hesitated. It's not like he could say, *make sure they don't find out you're a Silver,* in broad daylight. "Well… about *you*."

"Yeah, well, that's easier said than done."

Eli's eyes went wild, searching mine and he grabbed my wrist.

"I just mean that they're both curious about me already."

"Why? What happened? Did they see something?"

"Not exactly. Aaron is suspicious of why I was Chosen, since I'm clearly not servant material. He said Jayce hand-picked me."

"He *what*? Why?"

"I have no idea." I shrugged. "And when I confronted Jayce-"

"You did what?" Eli jumped up from the bench. "Do you have a death wish?" he said under his breath to not draw attention.

I pulled him by the arm and made him sit back down. "I told you, he's not as bad as people think."

"What did he say then, when you confronted him?"

"He denied that he had anything to do with it, and then he insulted me, actually," I chuckled at Eli's expression. "And then disappeared."

I didn't mention that we had spoken afterwards after dinner, or that he had brought me food and treated me kindly. I wasn't really sure what that was all about yet, and I was worried about what Eli would say. I didn't want to look stupid in front of him.

"Well, that doesn't bode well." He leaned back and looked straight ahead.

"I know. That's why I need your help getting me out of there."

"To go where?"

"Can't I 'serve' you?" I used air quotes, knowing full well he would never actually make me serve him.

"If it was any other household, maybe, but not the Starrs. And it doesn't matter that you're my sister, because technically you're a Commoner, and I'm really not even supposed to consider you family anymore. It could put both of our lives in jeopardy."

"I can't stay," I looked down at my hands in my lap. "They'll figure it out eventually, especially with my birthday coming up, and then what?"

"I don't know," he sighed. "We'll think of something."

I nodded and my heart felt a little lighter. Just knowing I had Eli on my side, that I wasn't alone, was enough for now.

"So tell me about Dad."

CHAPTER 19

I had been dreading that question. I wasn't sure Eli would understand the relationship I now had with our father. I didn't really hold any bitterness towards him for what he had become. Maybe it was my guilt over the entire thing, but I was never able to bring myself to hate him, even if I had to grow up too fast to make up for his lack of parenting.

"Dad is…" I struggled to find words. "Dad is alone now. I'm worried about him, but he'll find a way to survive."

How could I tell him the truth? That after that night our father had become a shell of himself. That his sister had to scrounge for scraps in the village as a young child, slipping back to her home in the dark, terrified and hungry. I didn't want him to pity me. My past made me who I am, and I wasn't ashamed of it. I couldn't stand the look on Eli's face if he ever found out how bad it had been for us while he grew up never having to worry where his next meal was coming from.

There had been times when he was downright cruel to me, in his darkest moments. Stumbling home after finding the bottom of a bottle, he would yell and scream, blaming me for our troubles. He had been right, of course, but that hadn't made it hurt any less. But the good times far outweighed the bad, and although we had next to nothing, I remembered my childhood as fondly as I could considering the circumstances.

"Gods, Willow, that sounds bleak. What is it that you're not saying there?"

Of course Eli could see right through me.

I sighed. "Dad never really recovered after you were taken away and Mom was…was…" I didn't have to say it out loud. He knew what had happened.

Eli grabbed my hand and gave it a squeeze.

"He didn't do much by way of raising me. For a while he made sure I had enough to eat and was getting to school on time, but once I became more self-sufficient, he shut down. He drinks too much, and doesn't really work at all. He did his best, Eli!" I finished as I saw the look concerned look on Eli's face turn to anger.

"His best? I can read between the lines here, Wil. He's a drunk that left you to bear the burden not only of losing your family, but also taking care of yourself and your useless father when you were just a child."

"It wasn't like that, Eli, please! Please don't think of

him with anger. Yes, things were difficult. But he had lost his son, and seen his wife murdered in front of him. And every day, I looked more and more like her. It was enough to break anyone. And I might have lacked a real parent to care for me, but I never lacked love. I don't hate him for it, Eli, and if I don't, then you have no right to either."

Eli bowed his head and took a few breaths, trying to calm himself down. I appreciated the concern for my well-being, but I was grown now. I was almost twenty, and had done a fine job of taking care of myself all these years. He didn't have to make me feel like such a child. Any anger he felt at my situation was years too late.

"You don't have the right to judge us, Eli. To judge him. You might have been there, seen what they did, but afterwards you came back here, and were raised a Mystic. You don't know what it's like to go hungry, what it's like to have barely enough water to drink, let alone clean yourself. You just don't *know*!"

"Willow. How did he provide you with food? With clothing? You said he didn't work-where did you get enough coin to survive?"

Not the direction I wanted this conversation to go in. I stood up abruptly. I was wasting time here, and I had to get back to the house soon.

"We did what we had to in order to survive, Eli! Let's just leave it at that. I didn't realize I was in for a scolding when I found you!"

Eli looked at me for a few seconds and then burst out laughing. "There's that temper I missed so much. For a second there I thought you had lost your spark."

I smiled a little and sat back down.

"I'm sorry your life has been so difficult. If I could have changed that, I would. But it was my fault the Mystics came to us that night, and I couldn't risk them finding you guys again. They would have killed all of us if they had found me a second time."

Apparently the Knights were all really good at feeling guilty.

He continued. "I knew the consequences of running away from school. I could have held on a little longer. Once I had been fully trained and graduated, I would have been able to visit without anyone noticing. I could have been better at hiding my sympathy for Commoners while still taking care of you guys. But you sounded so sad in your letters, and I missed you all so much. I shouldn't have come to you. I shouldn't have left the region. I shouldn't have...

"Eli," I interrupted. "You were a boy. How could you have known what would happen? Neither of us could have imagined the consequences."

Eli forced the tears back and gave me a weak smile.

"When did you get so grown up, sis?" he asked, ruffling my hair.

I laughed, and we talked a little about the village and what life was like for me, but I was curious about Eli, too. I didn't really know how he had been raised.

"What have you been doing, Eli? You look good, well fed and healthy. You must be doing well for yourself. What's life been like for you here?"

"It has its ups and downs. I work for the police force

here. Not as an enforcer, of course. Those are all from the Lapis region, but I'm a detective, so I help solve crimes and make things safer. That's how I met Lilliana, actually. She was a healer on a case I was working and we became fast friends. She's good people, Wil. If you need anything and you can't find me, ask for her. She can help you."

I started to answer, but Eli had glanced at his watch and jumped up from the bench.

"You should get back before they notice you're missing," he urged.

I let out a heavy sigh. Now that I'd found Eli, I didn't want to leave him, even though I knew he was right. We would have to be careful going forward. It didn't matter that I served the Starrs now. Eli would still be punished for showing me any kind of sympathy or helping me in any way.

"How will I find you again?"

"Just come to the bookstore. I can see it from my window. I live right across the street, just there. See it? Three windows in from the left, in case you ever need me. I'll notice you at the shop, don't worry." He smiled. "It's going to be okay. We'll figure something out."

I nodded and wrapped my arms around his neck. "I missed you," I whispered into his ear.

"Missed you too, sis." He gave me a squeeze and then we both let go. "Stay safe." He ruffled my hair and I pulled out of his grasp laughing.

He started toward the bookshop and my heart ached to see him go.

"See you soon," I called after him.

He waved without looking back and I turned to head back to the Starr house. I simultaneously felt like the whole world was right again, and like my heart wouldn't survive the time apart.

I forced myself to look away from Eli's receding form and make my way back. My thoughts were swirling through my head like a swarm of butterflies. I barely got to the end of one before the next one interjected. But the one thought I kept coming back to was that *I'd found Eli,* actually found him, and my heart didn't know how to comprehend the joy it was feeling.

Even since that night, I had dreamed of that moment. Of seeing my brother again, holding him in my arms. I remembered a dozen things I had wanted to tell him when I saw him again. Years and years of memory, of life lived without him. And for him, life lived without me. I started making a mental note on the questions I wanted to ask him, to get to know him again. Did he still love sweets? Had he continued his sword training? Had he ever been in love? A life lived, and missed. He was family, and I barely knew him.

I turned up the next street, making my way back to the house. I wasn't paying attention, and I walked right into something solid. The familiar smell of citrus and vanilla sent a bolt of panic through me, and a pair of arms grabbed my shoulders to steady me.

I looked up and deep blue eyes met mine. His lips curled into a smile and his head cocked to one side as he looked at me. My heart leapt into my chest, and my abilities began to surface without control as my fight or flight response kicked in.

Jayce's deep, smooth voice sent shivers down my spine. "Oh Ms. Knight, what are we going to do with you?"

CHAPTER 20

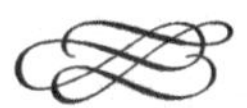

I took a deep breath, trying to get my emotions under control so my abilities wouldn't completely take over and expose me in the middle of the street. There was no way out of this, so it was time to play nice and hope things fell my way.

"I take it letting me go isn't an option?" I smiled and looked up at him with puppy dog eyes. I was shooting for sweet and innocent, but the way his brow furrow told me I may have missed the mark.

"You'd be correct." He grabbed me by the arm and started walking me back toward the house. "I've never met anyone with such little regard for their own well-being," he grumbled like I was a misbehaving child.

"Just because I take risks doesn't mean I don't understand the consequences," I said to his back.

He whirled on me, and I almost knocked into him. "You don't have a clue what you're risking, let alone the consequences of your actions." He kept his voice low, and I could feel his breath on my face. If looks could kill, surely I would have burst into flames on the spot.

My cheeks flushed and I realized that the street noise had completely disappeared, and everyone's eyes were glued to us. I wanted to melt into the pavement and disappear forever. I hated this much attention on me at the best of times, let alone when the most powerful Mystic in the world was yelling at me like a petulant child in front of the whole region. The Gods could smite me now, and I'd thank them for the kindness.

"Let's go," he said under his breath as he marched me through the street. I could only imagine what was going through everyone's minds. Hushed whispers followed in our wake and as much as I wanted to tell him he was wrong, there was one thing I wanted more: to get the heck out of sight.

As we reached the next street, I felt like I was in a haze. I'd been so happy just moments ago, sitting with my brother again, only for everything to come crashing down once more. He pulled me behind him as we crossed the street and started to make our way up the long incline to the house.

As we reached a large tree halfway to the house, I realized I needed to start doing damage control. He was angry and I had no idea if he was going to march me straight to Aaron or torture me himself.

"I'm sorry," I stumbled over the words.

"Think you can say it like you mean it?" He let go of

my arm and turned to face me under the canopy of the tree.

"Are you going to tell Aaron?"

"Do you know what Aaron would do if he found out you were sneaking out of the house?" He let out a heavy sigh and folded his arms over his chest.

"Yeah, I have a pretty good idea." The memory of him trapping me in my own personal hell of darkness flashed through my mind.

"What could be so important to risk his wrath?" His blazing eyes pierced into mine like I was a small child.

Lie, said the voice in my head.

"I've barely had the chance to explore my new home." I met his eyes, knowing full well people believed you more when you didn't look away from them. "I wanted to learn more about this region and what it's like beyond the four walls of your house."

He took a step toward me, so we were only inches apart. He towered over me and as he leaned in, the soft, sweet scent of his cologne wrapped around me.

"Bullshit." His eyes bore into mine and I felt my mouth go dry. I never understood why people thought he was so intimidating, until right now. It's like he could see right through me to every secret I was so desperate to keep hidden.

I opened my mouth to defend myself, but for the first time, no words came to mind.

"I don't think you care at all what the Scarlet region has to offer." He smirked and pressed closer, forcing me to step back until I was up against the trunk of the tree. "I think you're looking for something, or some*one*." His eyes searched my face for any reaction. I could feel the blood drain from my cheeks, and my heart start to thump wildly in my chest.

"What's wrong? Can't think of a convincing lie?" He closed the gap between us and placed a hand on the trunk next to my head. He was so close, and his scent surrounded me, making it hard to think. A sharp chill ran through me, like I'd been dunked in a frozen lake. Jayce knew too much about me and my motivations. And that's when it hit me, like a lightning strike. I might not know much about him, but I did know that I wasn't the only one under this tree with secrets.

"I think you have me confused with yourself." I watched him carefully.

The corner of his eyes twitched, and his jaw flexed. "What's that supposed to mean?" His eyes turned a deep blue, and I knew I needed to play my cards carefully or he might decide to kill me right then and there.

I raised a brow and placed my hand on his chest, forcing him to take a step back. "I'm not the one sneaking around alleys and meeting with people in secret."

For one quick moment, his stare went blank, then confused, then murderous. He was definitely caught off guard by my words, and rightfully so.

"I don't know what you're talking about." He took another step back.

"Oh, but I think you do." I stepped into his space now that he was on the defense. "You held this up as if it was some kind of key." I pulled my necklace out from under my clothes for him to see, daring him to deny it. "Why? What is it?"

He opened his mouth, but I interrupted him. "And don't say it's about family and loyalty and all that. I want the truth."

"You don't know what you're talking about." His eyes blazed with a quiet fury, and his hands were tight in fists. "And if you have any sense in that skull of yours, you'll keep your mouth shut."

"Or what? You said you'd never hurt me." I squared my shoulders. "Or are you just like all the other Mystics- liars and bastards?"

"Watch your tongue," he snarled and came forward, pushing me back against the tree, looming over me. "While I don't take pleasure in the pain of others, Aaron does, and he has no mercy."

"You wouldn't." I exhaled the words, truly afraid I'd pushed him too far.

"Don't test me, Ms. Knight," he said through gritted teeth.

"I'll keep your secret if you keep mine." My voice came out as a whimper, and I hated how weak I sounded.

"Under one condition." He let out a heavy sigh and his features softened. It appeared that the storm was over.

"I'm not going to like it am I?" I looked up at him and his eyes met mine. They were soft, pleading and my heart gave a gentle squeeze that I tried to ignore.

"You have to stop sneaking out of the house. It's too dangerous."

"Why do you care what happens to me?" My heart felt

like it was going to beat out of my chest. I wasn't sure if I was reacting in fear to the thought that he might kill me, or if I was thrilled at the idea that he cared about me. He was still standing close, *so close,* to me.

"Because you're too important." He placed his hand on my cheek and I couldn't stop the blush that rushed to my face. "And Aaron won't hesitate to destroy you if you give him a reason."

His words sunk into my bones and realization hit me like a ton of bricks. "So it's true then?" I pulled his hand from my face, and it fell to his side. "You…you did handpick me." I could barely get the words out of my mouth.

His eyes fell from mine and he nodded once as he took a step away from me. I immediately missed his closeness.

"Why?" I slumped against the tree. Everything Aaron said was true.

He shook his head as he took another step away and turned his back on me.

"Jayce, please." I reached out, touching his shoulder so he would turn around to look at me.

"The less you know, the better." He pulled out of my grasp and faced me. "You have a deal. I'll keep your secret if you keep mine," he said without looking at me. There was no more anger, no more concern, just indifference as he stared at the leaves above our heads.

"Deal."

"Let's get back before someone notices you're missing." He motioned for me to follow him as he started up the street toward the house.

I had more questions than ever, and I had no idea what my next step should be. But there was one thing I knew for certain: Despite having absolute dicks for parents, Jayce Starr was not the monster people made him out to be.

CHAPTER 21

"Mom?" I called out. Her chestnut hair flipped over her shoulders as she turned to look at me. Her violet eyes, so similar to my own, captured mine, making me freeze in my steps. "Is it really you?" I croaked.

Her kind face turned dark and angry. "You did this to me, my dear Willow." The light, carefree voice I once remembered now turned stoic and emotionless.

"No," I shook my head. "I didn't want this," I forced out, trying to shove away the tears that begged to be let free.

A small, lost smile tilted on her pink lips. "You had abilities that got me killed. That is on you."

I opened my mouth, but no words escaped. I had nothing to say. She was right. It was my job to build back the family I destroyed.

"I'm sorry, Mom." With those three words, my dam broke. Tears streamed down my face uncontrollably.

"My dear girl. Don't apologize for something that's already

been done. You can't change what you've already ruined." She shrugged and her body began to disappear from my sight.

"Don't leave me again, please," I begged. The closer I walked towards her, the faster she began to dissipate.

"You did this," she stated.

"No!" I screamed, hoping that she could come back, and I could hug her and apologize again until she forgave me.

I shot up in bed, drenched in sweat. *It was just a dream.*

"It was just a dream," I panted.

I sat up, heart still racing, and looked at the clock on the nightstand. It was five in the morning. I threw myself back down on my pillow and stared at the ceiling, trying to slow my heart rate. Rationally, I knew it was just a dream, but I couldn't shake the feeling of guilt. It might not have been my fault that my family was torn apart, but Eli never would have come back to visit if I hadn't sent him letter after letter asking him to. It was my fault he was there that night.

The memory of my mother lying on the floor, blood pooling around her, made my stomach churn and no matter how many deep breaths I took, it wasn't enough. I needed some fresh air. I jumped out of bed and threw on some clothes. Leaving my room behind, I made my way to the garden between the house and the arena.

The moment I stepped outside, the cold air hit me like a wave. My skin prickled and as I exhaled, I could see my breath on the chilly morning air. I walked through the garden and turned off the stone path, making my way to the wall at the edge of the garden. The top of the wall came up to my ribcage and I hoisted myself up with little effort. Wrapping my arms around myself, I shivered as I took another deep breath and tried to let my nightmare go.

It was still dark enough that I felt secluded, but just light enough to see the houses below and the tiny streetlights. It was quiet, peaceful, and exactly what I needed. Which was more than I could say about the last few days.

After Jayce and I agreed to keep each other's secrets, we'd made our way back to the house and went our separate ways. Aaron had kept me busy with preparation for the Gala. I wasn't sure what Jayce got up to, but I saw him every day around the house now. I got the feeling he was keeping an eye on me and making sure I wasn't sneaking out anymore.

And honestly, even if I'd wanted to, I was too exhausted after spending every waking hour being worked to the bone to leave. I barely made it to my bed every night before passing out, only to be haunted by my nightmares. They'd been getting worse and more frequent. I was worried it was because my birthday was around the corner and my abilities were on the verge of coming into full power.

"Ms. Knight?" Jayce came up beside me, his brow furrowed. "Everything alright?" His worried expression didn't go unnoticed, and I wondered why he cared so much. I also couldn't help but notice that I liked the fact that he worried about me.

"Just couldn't sleep." I looked away from him and back

to the view. The sun was still a way off from rising, but I could feel the shift in the air.

"That makes two of us." He smirked and leaned against the wall next to me.

I fought the urge to tell him to leave me alone, that I'd rather be by myself. But now that we'd come to a sort of understanding, it wasn't so bad having him around. It was almost like he was a friend. Almost. I just had to be careful.

"Anything in particular keeping you from your sleep?" He queried.

"Just a bad dream."

I could feel him watching me out of the corner of my eye, waiting for me to go on. But there was no way I was sharing my nightmare with him, or anyone for that matter.

"You can talk to me. You know that, right?"

"Can I, though?" I kept my eyes on the lights below, and somehow not meeting his gaze made it a lot easier to talk.

"I know I may not be your favorite person, but everyone should have someone they can talk to."

"Do you?" I turned to look at him. "Have someone to talk to?"

"I have my brother," he said not meeting my gaze.

A snort-laugh escaped my throat. "I may be fairly new here, but there is no way Aaron is your person."

"Maybe you're right." He looked at me and his smirk sent a shiver through my abdomen. *Get a grip, Willow.* "So how about I tell you something and you tell me something?"

"Alright, you first." I swung my feet up onto the wall and hugged my knees. There was so much about him that just didn't add up, and a thrill settled in my chest at the thought of adding to his puzzle.

"I hate the Gala."

"What?" I nearly yelled. "You're joking." I lowered my voice.

He shook his head. "It's the same thing every year. Same people, same boring stories. And for what?"

"Wow, I have to say, I did not see that coming. Everyone seems to be over the moon about the Gala."

"There are more important things in life than fancy parties," he shrugged. "Your turn." He met my eyes and for some reason, I felt a rush of embarrassment.

"Err...I don't know." I shrugged.

Taking a deep breath, I inhaled and caught the scent of sandalwood, earthy and familiar, and felt at ease. *Why does he always have to smell, and look, so good? I'd like to see what he looks like when he first wakes up in the morning and hasn't brushed his teeth or combed his hair yet. It was annoying how put together he always seems.*

Jayce chuckled, and my eyes widened. I wondered if I just said that out loud. "What?" I demanded.

"Nothing." He looked down at the grass and kicked at the dirt.

"I met a Gold the other day. She's a healer, and reads auras."

"Was she the first Gold you've ever met?"

I leveled my eyes on him. "No, they used to come to town every weekend when I was a kid." I rolled my eyes. "Of course she was the first. I've seen them work at the Choosing ceremony every year, but I've never personally spoke to one, or had one comment on my aura."

"And what did she say about your aura?" He cocked his head to the side and his eyes searched my face.

This was dangerous territory. No way was I admitting that she'd never seen anything like it. He didn't need another reason to wonder about me being unique.

"She said I had the aura of royalty," I smirked.

"I doubt that," he shook his head.

"Your turn. What was growing up the son of the Scarlet leaders like?" I asked.

"Well... My parents had travel to different regions a lot when I was a kid, so often that I could never really keep track of them. Aaron will get the title soon, my dad just hasn't made it official yet, so growing up he would go with him to travel all over and learn how to be diplomatic."

I snorted. "He wasn't a very good student, obviously."

Jayce smiled. "He can turn on the charm when he needs to, and he genuinely wants to make life the best it can be for the Scarlets. But he wasn't around much as a kid either, and now he's busy handling all that responsibility, so we don't talk much. I'm probably closer to Jaxtyn than I am to Aaron. I definitely know him better, anyway."

For some reason I expected him to be close with his family. I assumed that if you had all the money and power in the world, you'd also be free to keep your family whole and close.

"I've been such a shweed," I admitted guiltily. "I didn't realize that you could have it all and still not have your family."

"Did you just say shweed?"

I nodded, "Shit head and a weed."

He laughed- an actual, full-hearted, crisp laugh. It made me smile in return. I liked hearing it.

"You're different, Ms. Knight." Those words made my smile falter, and he noticed. "That isn't a bad thing."

I shrugged. "I'm used to being different."

"Then why does it bother you?"

I looked out over the valley. The sky was starting to fade to a light blue. "I'm not used to being noticed. I miss being invisible. In my region, no one cared about me. Except for my dad." My heart squeezed and I closed my eyes, trying to push the pain back down.

"You miss him?" he guessed.

I nodded. "I don't know how he's doing now. If he's eating, if he's still drinking. He needs me, and now I'm here."

"I can't help but feel somewhat responsible." He sighed and folded his arms over his chest. "I can send food for your father, if it'll help put your mind at ease." He offered with a small smile, turning towards me and I couldn't stop the grin that pulled at my lips.

"Why would you do that for me?" I asked.

He shrugged. "To show you that you can trust me."

Would it work? How could I trust someone who

belonged to the same people that had torn my family apart? My father needed this food because of people like Jayce. Or at least, people like Jayce's family.

"You're not like the other Mystics I've known."

"You're not the first person to say that." He sighed and pursed his lips like he was sick of hearing that he was different. I understood the feeling.

"Would you rather be more like the rest of them?" I looked toward the town down below, thinking about all the Mystics who lived down there, and wondered if there were more like Jayce and Eli out there.

"No, but it'd be nice to be invisible sometimes." His eyes met mine and I could swear at that moment he knew about my abilities.

"What's the matter? Being wealthy, beautiful, and on top of the world isn't living up to expectations?" I tried to take the attention off of me and immediately regretted my words.

"Beautiful?" He cocked an eyebrow and smirked.

"Objectively, you're not the worst thing to look at." I tried to recover, but my cheeks felt like they were on fire. Thank the Gods it was still somewhat dark out.

"Careful Ms. Knight. You're dangerously close to giving me a compliment."

"Allow me to fix that," I rolled my eyes. "You're still a filthy Mystic."

A low chuckle rumbled through his chest. "I've never met anyone who hates Mystics more than you."

"Like anyone would ever be honest with you?" I shook my head. "The great and powerful Jayce."

"You're honest with me. A little too honest, sometimes."

"Yeah well, I don't have a lot to lose."

"Something tells me you have more to lose than you might realize."

Does he always have to be so cryptic? I wondered, and again he smirked like he could hear my thoughts. Was that a thing? Could Scarlets hear your thoughts? Ugh, I wished I'd paid more attention in school.

Lost in my thoughts about Mystic abilities, the silence stretched on, and still Jayce just stayed next to me as the sun started to rise. I'd never shared a sunrise with someone before and I had to admit, it wasn't totally awful.

"We should probably get going," he finally said. "I'm sure we both have lots to do before the Gala tomorrow night." He held out his hand to help me down from the wall and I took it on instinct.

"Ugh, don't remind me."

"Try and get your work done quickly. I'd love to see you tonight."

I froze, unsure how to respond.

"In the simulation, I mean," he clarified.

My face was hot as I nodded and left as quickly as I could.

CHAPTER 22

Since the Gala was just a day away, my to-do list was extra long. When I got back to my room after the conversation with Jayce, I had a list waiting for me.

1. *Polish the staircase. I want it shining this time, no scruffs or I'll be sure you're sorry*
2. *Scrub the floor in the dining hall*
3. *Make sure the chairs are clean and lint free*
4. *Polish the silverware*
5. *Clean the dishes*

The list went on and on. I wasn't sure if I would finish it in time, but I was going to try and see Jayce again tonight. In the simulator. For research purposes, of course. Was I lying to myself? Maybe.

The morning conversation in the garden had unnerved

me. It was frustrating to feel this way about a Mystic, especially a Mystic from this particular family. But I was struggling to see the bad in him, the evil that the rest of his family carried. I thought back to all the things I knew about him, and it just didn't make sense.

First of all, he treated me like a person, which was far more than I could say about his brother or parents. He said please, and seemed uncomfortable bossing me around. Almost apologetic. Second, he had the same necklace as my mother. The necklace that people believed was an old relic of the Silvers. And he was using it for some secret purpose, or at least that's what it seemed like when I saw him in the alleyway at the secret door. And lastly, my gut told me I could trust him. And I always trusted my gut.

As I was polishing the silverware, Aaron walked into the dining room to check on the progress of the setup. The Gala was turning out to be a beautiful affair. There were tables covered in deep scarlet tablecloths lined with shiny gold threads. At the center of each table would be a towering centerpiece, delivered tomorrow morning. There was a stage at the end of the room which would elevate whoever was standing on it enough to see the whole room. On the stage was a long table, with an ornate golden bowl sitting in the center of it. I wasn't sure what that was for, but whatever it was, it couldn't be good. I watched Aaron inspect the bowl before covering it up carefully with a another of the scarlet tablecloths.

"Make sure that silverware shines, Commoner," Aaron

sneered as he walked past. "And we counted all of those pieces, so don't try to steal one."

I didn't bother with a response. As soon as he was out the door, I stuck my tongue out in his direction and got back to work, polishing quickly. I wasn't going to let him get to me. I couldn't let him win.

Later on, I was grabbing some food from the kitchens when Alice popped up behind me.

"Hi Ms. Willow!"

I knew I was too used to living her when I didn't even jump at her appearance.

"Hi Alice. How are you today?" I was in an excellent mood, and I hoped she wasn't here to dampen my spirits.

"I'm fine, thank you! Mr. Jayce sent me to remind you that should you finish your work early, he'd like to see you in the simulation tonight."

I rolled my eyes at her, and she gave me a small smile. Sometimes I forgot she wasn't a real person, but in this case it was obvious. Her programming didn't allow her to say anything, or do anything, negative about her bosses. Another human would have given me a sympathetic look.

"You can tell Mr. Jayce that while I am but a lowly Commoner, my brain is capable of retaining information, and I don't need him to remind me of his request."

"Should I relay your message word for word, Ms. Willow?"

Ha. Poor Alice was not interested in delivering my attitude-filled message. I took pity on her and reworded my response. "You can just tell him I remember, but I can't promise anything. I still have a lot left on my to-do list."

"Mr. Jayce said he knew you would say that, and requested that I take a look at what was remaining and delegate a few things to other servants in order to hurry you along."

Unbelievable.

"Alice, I don't need their help. No one else should have to do my work for me."

"We're all happy to serve the Starr family."

Creepy, but she was right. Everyone I had spoken to so far had genuinely enjoyed being here. I always thought that once the people who were chosen got to their new homes, they'd realize what a farce it was. But apparently, they never lost their excitement. "Ok. Here's my list. How about you take the last two and pass them on to the others, and I'll polish the staircase." I felt bad enough letting someone else do my work. I wasn't going to make them polish the damn staircase, as tempting as that was. Plus, the other tasks included being in the laundry room and the gardens, and I thought they were less likely to run into Aaron there. I wasn't sure how he would react to finding someone else doing my work.

I left for the simulation later that night, reeking of floor polish and absolutely exhausted. As I punched in the code to enter, I saw Jayce waiting for me on the other side of the door.

"Glad you could make it, Ms. Knight."

"You didn't really give me much of a choice."

"Regardless, I'm glad you're here." Jayce flashed me a smile and then motioned towards the machine. "What'll be- controls, or simulation?"

"Simulation," I said, surprising myself, and Jayce.

"Ms. Knight, you are just full of surprises. Please, choose your weapon."

I stepped into the simulation room with the same weapon I had chosen the last time- the sword with the gemstone handle. It felt good in my hands, and I realized that somehow, I had missed holding it.

"Ok, Ms. Knight," Jayce's voice came from the speaker, "We're going to just do what we did last time. I'll keep it on an easy level, and I want you to try as best as you can to remember what happens in there, so we can talk about it afterwards."

We'll see, I thought to myself, and then the simulation began.

I was ready to see my mom, had been mentally preparing myself for it all day if I was honest, but she didn't appear this time. Instead, a man I didn't know stood before me. He was tall, almost unnaturally so. His skin was fair, and his hair a shocking black, darker than the night sky on a starless night. He smiled, and a chill ran down my spine. I could feel his hatred, and his malice. And then he stepped aside, and Jayce was lying on the floor behind him, dying.

"No!" I screamed. *It's not real. It's just a simulation.* I fought as hard as I could to leave my powers tucked away, but I could feel them rushing to the surface, threatening to burst out at any moment. I surged forward, knowing if I didn't fight this man, Jayce would die.

He parried my first blow, and his fist collided with my face. It might not be real, but I *felt* that.

"Ms. Knight, are you alright? The readings out here are doing something I've never seen, and the simulation isn't responding to my commands."

"Fine," I gritted through my teeth. As I kept fighting the stranger, I saw the Jayce figure on the floor take his last breath. *Oh, now I'm angry.*

"Ms. Knight, I need you to leave the simulation. End it. Something's wrong, and I can't guarantee your safety."

I heard the stranger chuckle. "Oh, poor Scarlet. He can't help you now."

Could he hear Jayce on the speaker? Or was he talking about the fake Jayce lying on the floor?

"Mystics always think they have complete control, but it's so easy to step in and take it from them. They never see it coming."

"Jayce," I yelled. "I want to get out!"

"Silly girl, don't you understand? You belong to me now."

My abilities rushed to my aid the moment fear entered my gut as I realized this guy wasn't a part of the simulation. He stepped forward and raised his hands, and darkness rushed around me, seemingly emanating from the man. I'd seen darkness before, the kind that used to make my street look like an old-fashioned photograph, everything a shade of grey. The kind that brought back every memory I had shoved deep down within myself. This wasn't like that. It was beyond that, a darkness so deep that it left me paralyzed, and came with a hopelessness that made me want to give up and let it take over. I felt a surge of power I couldn't explain, beyond anything I had felt before. I wanted to give in, to relax into the darkness that so eagerly kissed up against my skin as close as it could, whispering excitement into my ears. It was a best friend that I kept pushing away, but it wouldn't stop until I became who it wanted me to be. My abilities didn't care about Jayce, or anyone else for that matter. They didn't react to seeing his body lying broken in front of me. They cared only about protecting me, and they acted on solely the anger and revenge I felt from within. They burst out of me in a ball of light, breaking through the darkness.

A showering of sparks fell over me as the simulation ended and Jayce ripped the door open. I collapsed into his arms.

"What happened?" I asked him, panting heavily.

"I don't know. Are you alright? You're so pale." He held my face in his hands, staring at me intently, trying to see if I had any injuries.

"I'm fine," I answered. And I was. Now that I was out of the simulation, the fear had left me, and I could think clearly again. I wasn't hurt, but I certainly wasn't going to be doing the simulation again any time soon.

Jayce laughed. "I won't make you do this again, ever." Did I say that out loud?

"What did you see in there?"

"There was a man. He talked to me...He said he was controlling the simulation."

"Impossible."

"Is it? You said it wasn't responding."

"I...I'm not sure. How did you get it to stop?"

That, I'm keeping to myself. "No idea. The light burst, and then you came through the door."

Jayce ran a hand through his hair. "Ok. I think we've seen enough of the simulation for the night." He walked over to where my sword had fallen when I collapsed, and placed it back with the other weapons. "I'll walk you to your room."

He took the stairs with me. I wasn't sure if he did it for my benefit, or if he wasn't willing to trust the machinery again just yet, but either way we walked to my room via the stairwell. When we got to my door, he paused, rocking on the balls of his feet and looking awkward.

"Will you be alright?" he asked.

"I've been through worse," I said, trying to give him a brave smile.

"Alice," Jayce said, and then turned to her when she appeared at his side. "Ms. Knight could use some food. Could you bring her up some dinner, and some extra sweets for dessert?"

"Of course, Mr. Jayce."

Jayce turned back to me, and placed a hand gently on my cheek. "Finish it all, Ms. Knight."

He slipped back into the stairwell and out of sight.

CHAPTER 23

I went through the next day on autopilot. Thankfully there wasn't too much on my list, since most of the Gala had already been set up throughout the week. All this work for a few hours seemed pointless to me, and it was nice to know I wasn't the only one who felt that. Jayce was surprising in more ways than one.

I thought about the night before, and what had happened in the simulation. I never wanted to go back in there, but I was also curious. Who was that man? And what had really happened? The day passed in a blur as I remained lost in thought.

I made my way back to my room early. I was excited to relax for once, and have some free time to myself while everyone else attended the Gala.

I stripped out of my work clothes and made my way to the bathroom to take a hot shower and wash away the day.

My dream had left a shadow on my heart, but after talking with Jayce this morning it was a little easier to bear.

Asking the shower to turn on, I stepped inside. The hot water felt like heaven. It still blew my mind that they never ran out of hot water here, and I could take a shower for as long as I wanted. Ducking my head under the water, I closed my eyes, and in the darkness of my mind, a pair of blue eyes and a smirk filled my vision.

My eyes shot open and I shook my head. There was no way I could let Jayce get under my skin. He was still a Scarlet, a Mystic, and he was still the reason I was here. It didn't matter that he treated me like a person. He was still a part of the system that destroyed my family. He was still a member of the family that had actively played a part in their destruction.

"Get a grip, Willow," I scolded myself again, and pushed him from my mind. Instead, I focused on whether or not I could convince the kitchen to let me have a taste of everything they were serving tonight. So far, I hadn't come across a pastry, loaf of bread, or slice of meat that I wasn't absolutely in love with. I swear, if I didn't know better, I'd think the cooks were magicians.

I rinsed my hair out and washed the soap off my body, then shut off the water and hopped out of the shower. As I wrapped a towel around my body and walked back into the bedroom, I nearly jumped out of my skin.

"By the Gods, Alice. You scared the crap out of me!"

"My apologies," she said looking me up and down. "Good! You've already showered."

"I thought we discussed- " I froze midsentence. "Wait,

why do you care that I've showered already?" I furrowed my brow as I stared at her.

"I'm here to help you get ready for the Gala."

A nervous laugh bubbled out of me. "I'm not going to the Gala."

"Oh my, I take it you didn't see the message from Aaron?" She crossed the room and picked up the tablet.

There was a message on the front of the screen.

See you tonight. Do us both a favor and make sure you're presentable.

I looked up from the message to Alice, who gave me an apologetic smile.

"He sent me to assist you."

"I thought the Gala was a Mystic-only event?" I was still in disbelief. He'd made it clear on numerous occasions that I was about appealing to him as a pile of crap. And now he wanted me at his fancy party? Why?

"Nonsense," she waved me off. "Don't you want to go and enjoy all your hard work?"

"Not really." I crossed the room and tossed the tablet onto the bed.

"I'm afraid your attendance isn't optional."

"So you weren't really sent here to assist me, were you?" I leveled my eyes on hers. "You're here to make sure I go."

"Aaron has been working hard to bring all the regions together, and your presence is meant to show everyone that we need *all* the regions working together, in harmony."

"I have a hard time believing Aaron cares about bringing us all together."

"Regardless, he has requested your presence, and we're already running late." She moved across the room and pulled the chair out from the desk. "Now sit."

"Whatever," I sighed. "Let's get this over with."

"Close your eyes. When I'm finished you can look," she ordered.

I nodded and closed my eyes. I wasn't a fan of getting dressed up. A part of me felt guilty for the Commoners who would never see a nice shirt or clean pair of pants in their lifetime, and here I was getting dolled up for a Gala.

I felt something on my eyelid, and I immediately opened them. "Willow, please hold still and stop opening your eyes, we don't have all night." She glared, clearly annoyed at me for making her pause her work.

"What are you doing?" I asked.

"Just a little bit of makeup. Aaron wants you to look your best."

"Oh," I mumbled. I never had it applied before, because Commoners barely had access to food, let alone frivolous beauty items. "So, it just makes me look prettier or what?" I raised a brow.

"It just enhances the beauty you already have."

I was curious about what the makeup would look like. It felt uncomfortable, stiff on my skin, and I couldn't imagine it actually did anything to enhance my beauty. But the soft, powdery brush strokes did feel nice.

"Are you done yet?" I groaned impatiently.

"Not yet, we need to deal with your hair." She pulled at the wet stands.

"Good luck with that," I chuckled, keeping my eyes closed. My hair took forever to dry and was a tangle of knots after I showered. I leaned back in the chair as Alice got to work, enjoying the feel of someone else doing my hair for once.

I let my mind wander as she dried, combed, pinned, curled, and sprayed my hair. After what felt like only minutes, she placed her hands on my shoulders.

"All done."

"Already?" I opened my eyes and touched my hair. It was dry and styled perfectly over my shoulder. "Where have you been all my life?"

"Now for the dress." Alice rushed me out of the chair before I could really get a good look at my makeup, and opened the closet. Inside hung a red dress made of satin.

"It's beautiful." I stepped forward and ran my fingers over the fabric. "But I could never wear this." I turned toward Alice.

"Of course you can." She pulled the dress down and handed it to me. "Now go put it on."

I stared at her for a long moment, wondering what she would do if I threw the dress in the shower. She grabbed my arm and placed the dress in my hand. She pushed me toward the bathroom and closed the door.

I looked at myself in the mirror and had to admit, the makeup was stunning and much softer than it felt. I still looked like myself for the most part, but my skin looked smooth, and as soft as the dress I was holding. My dark hair was curled, reaching my elbow, and my violet eyes stood out against the black on my eyelashes.

I looked down at the dress in my hands and sighed. "I guess there's a first time for everything." I let my towel drop to the floor and slipped the dress on over my head. The satin hugged my body and was hands-down the most luxurious thing to ever touch my skin.

"Need any help?" Alice called through the door.

"All good," I said taking one last look at myself and making my way back into the room.

"Ms. Willow," she gasped. "You look breathtaking."

I smirked and looked down at the dress. I hated to admit it, but it actually felt good to be dressed up.

"Come," she motioned me forward. Grabbing me by the shoulders, she positioned me in front of the mirror so I could take in my whole look.

The dress was floor-length, making me look taller than I was, and it hugged me in all the right places without being too tight. A high collar wrapped my neck. I liked that it didn't have any sleeves, so it felt moveable if it had to be. I turned from side to side, the fabric swirling around me and peppering my body with soft, sensual kisses.

"Ready?" Alice said holding the door open.

"As I'll ever be." I looked between her and the mirror, and then made my way to the door.

She led me to the elevator and pressed the button for the top floor. As the elevator started to rise, I could hear the music playing, and my heart felt like it would beat out of my chest. I was so not ready to be this on display.

The elevator signaled our arrival and the doors swung open. There were people everywhere, all dressed in their best. The red curtains I'd dug out of the basement were hung in front of every window, from floor to ceiling. Soft, tiny lights hung from the ceiling mimicking the night sky and giving the entire floor an intimate feel.

"Enjoy the Gala," Alice smiled and disappeared without another word.

Shoot. Now what was I supposed to do? I looked around the crowd of people.

Sticking to the wall, I watched as people laughed, hugged, kissed, and shared stories. I couldn't help but smirk as I remembered Jayce saying that's all these parties were.

"Willow, is that you?" A chipper voice called my name. Lilliana made her way from the crowd to say hello.

I looked down at myself, and I was no longer in the satin dress. Lilliana and the others had all vanished. Instead, there were dozens of new people around me, and the atmosphere was electric, filled with a positive energy that seeped into my bones.

I felt more power coursing through my veins than I ever had. Golden rays of sunshine shone down on me, and it felt like the sun was handing me more power. All of the buildings around me looked to be made of ice, but as I walked closer, I realized it was crystal. As I looked around, I saw a palace sitting on top of a hill that overlooked all the other smaller homes below. It was the most beautiful thing I'd ever seen.

"How are you today?" A man approached me, and at first he was blurry. I blinked my eyes a few times, and his hazel eyes and cinnamon hair came into focus.

"I – um – I..." I stuttered, staring at him, not knowing who he was. His soft hand reached towards my own, grabbing it gently. I furrowed my eyebrow., The touch felt warm and... right.

"Low, it's me," he urged.

"I don't know..." I took a quick step back.

"A lot has happened, I know. That's why you need to rest." His eyes pierced mine with uncertainty.

"This can't be real," I murmured.

Everything around me began to blur again, and the familiar sounds of the Gala reached my ears. I felt the hardwood floor beneath my feet, and my ears started to ring as the penthouse reformed around me.

"Willow?" Lilliana's face came back into view, and she wore a concerned expression. "Are you alright?"

I shook off whatever that was and pulled my shoulder out from her grasp. "I'm fine, sorry. I'm just not used to... all this." I motioned around the room.

"Are you sure? Your aura completely changed for a second there!" Her eyes looked around the edges of me before she met my eyes again.

"Just a little overwhelmed," I smiled. "If you'll excuse me for a minute," I said over my shoulder as I crossed the room.

What the actual heck was happening to me? I thought the moment I was away from Lilliana. My abilities were all over the place lately, but visions? That was new and weird. I was seriously running out of time. My birthday coming up so soon.

As I pushed through the crowd, I promised myself I'd

go see Eli in the morning and we'd come up with a solid plan to get me out of here.

I finally made it across the room and away from searching eyes. I leaned against the wall and took a deep breath. This was going to be a long night.

CHAPTER 24

"Ms. Knight?" Jayce walked up next to me, and all I could do was stare at him. He wore a black suit with dark maroon trim. The jacket showed off his broad shoulders, and looked like it was made perfectly to fit him. And really, the whole suit was most likely custom made for him. I wasn't complaining.

"You look..." his eyes moved up and down the length of me.

"Different?" I supplied as I looked down at the red flowing dress.

"I was going to say stunning." His eyes reached mine and he smiled.

I could feel the blush creep up my chest and into my cheeks and I looked away from him toward the other guests. It didn't go unnoticed that most of the women in the room were eyeing him up and down. A small flicker of defiance sparked in my chest, and I turned to him. They may be staring at him, but he was looking at me and it had to drive them crazy.

"Careful, you wouldn't want someone to overhear you complimenting a Commoner. It'd be quite the scandal," I said looking out over the crowd of people.

The music shifted from an up-tempo beat to a soft, almost ethereal melody. Without the bass pumping through the room, the anxiety coursing through me settled ever so slightly.

"Then let's give them all a heart attack." He grabbed my hand and pulled me into the middle of the dancing guests.

A nervous laugh escaped my throat. "What the hell are you doing?" I said through gritted teeth and tried to pull my arm free.

"Dancing." He turned on the spot and the whisper of a smile touched his lips.

"Absolutely not." I started to take a step back when his arm slide around my waist and pulled me toward him.

My dress was so thin that I could feel the heat of him through our clothing, and my heart kicked up a notch.

"I...don't...erm...I'm not a dancer," I stumbled through my words as he pressed my body to his and grabbed my other hand.

"It's a good thing I am." The corner of his lips turned up as his eyes met mine.

He started to move us in a small circle, and I did my best to follow him. It was hard to focus on the dancing when it felt like everyone's eyes were on us. I couldn't help but wonder what Aaron would think. He was already suspicious of Jayce and I, and this was so not going to help the situation.

He spun me in a circle and pulled me back into his arms. "You're a natural." I could hear the smile in his voice.

"More like a natural at getting myself into ridiculous situations," I rolled my eyes, but my heart wasn't in it. It was hard to be annoyed when I was so distracted by his hand on my lower back.

A low chuckle rumbled through Jayce's chest and again I wondered how people could find him so intimidating. Sure, there was a fierceness to him that simmered under the surface, but I'd yet to see him treat anyone the way Aaron treats people.

"I have to admit, I was surprised to see you here tonight." He cocked his head to the side and looked down at me.

"Aaron didn't tell you?" A pang of unease shot through me. The fact that Jayce didn't know his brother basically forced me to be here wasn't a good sign. Aaron was up to something, and I really didn't want to have any part in it.

"Aaron's not big on sharing his plans with me." He shrugged as if he wasn't concerned.

"He requested that I attend, though it's not much of a request if I don't have a choice in the matter," I sighed.

"Odd. It's not uncommon for Commoners to attend Mystic events, but Aaron's never been keen on the idea." He frowned.

"Who knows why Aaron does anything he does." Jayce lifted his arm again and guided me through another spin. His hand left the small of my back for a fraction of a second, only to grab my hip and pull me back to him.

"Where did you learn to dance?" I asked changing the subject. Aaron was the last thing I wanted to be thinking about right now.

"I took lessons as a boy." He looked off into the distance as if he was remembering some long-lost memory. "My mother wanted me to be well rounded." He looked down at me and there was a sadness behind his eyes that I couldn't place.

We stood there starring at each other as the song came to an end. I had no idea what he was thinking and whether or not I should ask more about his mother or change the subject.

"Mr. Starr?" Alice appeared next to us and I nearly jumped out of my skin. I was never going to get used to her popping in and out of existence.

"What is it, Alice?" Jayce let his hands fall from me and turned to face her.

"There are some guests downstairs who require your attention," she smiled, and her pixel eyes blinked like she didn't have a care in the world.

"Very well, I'll be right down." He nodded to her, and she vanished once again.

He guided me off the dance floor and back to the wall where he'd found me. "Try not to have too much fun without me," he said raising his eyebrows.

"Wouldn't dream of it."

He disappeared into the elevator, and I was back to watching the guest mingle and interact with one another, without knowing why I was here. There was no way Aaron would make me attend the Gala just to people watch, so what did he want? How long was I going to have to stand here when all I wanted was to lay down and relax?

Another song started to play, and plates of food were carried around by the kitchen staff. As much as I wanted to grab some food, I couldn't bring myself to approach them. I felt way too guilty that I was here all dressed up while they were still working.

Maybe Aaron just wanted people to see me, like Alice suggested, to bring the regions together. I figured I'd done my part and I could make my exit. As I started to cross the room, someone clinked a glass and a hush fell over the crowd. Aaron stepped up onto the stage, holding a glass and looking even more pompous than he normally did.

"Thank you all for coming," he said. "It's wonderful to see so many familiar faces." He looked over the crowd waving to someone and nodding to another like he was some king surveying his subjects.

"I'd like to kick off the night with a ritual my father discontinued years ago." Aaron stepped up to the table on the stage and pulled the sheet back to reveal the golden bowl. A quiet murmur moved through the guests. Some seemed to recognize what the bowl was meant for, while others looked confused or excited.

"Some of our traditions have fallen away over the years, but tonight we bring them back," Aaron continued as he ran a finger around the rim of the bowl.

There was a whoop of applause and excitement from a few people toward the front of the room.

"Tonight, we honor the Gods that made us, and give thanks for the blood that runs through our veins."

At the mention of blood, I froze, and chills ran down my arms.

"If we could have the volunteers up here." Aaron motioned for people to join him. "And of course, you too Ms. Knight."

It took me half a second to process that he'd said my name, and then everything in me screamed *'run'*.

I turned away from the crowd and made a beeline for the elevator. Two men blocked my way and my abilities tingled along my skin. I tried to push past them, but they grabbed me by my arms and started to march me toward Aaron.

"Let go of me." I struggled against them, trying to pull myself free, but they held onto my arms with a death grip. I wanted to let my abilities take over so I could free myself, but in a room full of Mystics, it would surely mean death.

"Fear not, Ms. Knight. We only need a little blood from you." Aaron smiled, but there was a glint in his eye that sent a shiver down my spine.

As the other volunteers joined me on stage, everything went into slow motion. My heartbeat was in my ears and my mouth felt dry. My blood. They needed my *blood*. How did I get here? How is this happening?

I searched the crowd for Jayce. Maybe he could put a stop to this somehow, but he still wasn't back, and I was starting to wonder if Alice had been ordered to get Jayce out of the room.

"With each drop of lifeblood spilled we honor the Gods." Aaron picked up a dagger encrusted with different color stones, and I wanted to vomit.

I screamed at myself internally for getting myself into this situation. For not trying to escape sooner. I'd spent my whole life hiding who I really was, and it was all for nothing. Aaron was going to expose me in front of a room full of Mystics, and they wouldn't waste any time killing me.

Aaron held his hand over a bowl and pulled the dagger through his hand. Deep scarlet blood dripped from his hand into the bowl and every fiber of my being screamed for me to escape.

He handed the blade to a man with a green tunic and as he slid the blade across his palm, his Verdant blood joined Aaron's in the bowl. Next up was an old woman, in a sequined dress that changed colors depending on the light. She pulled the dagger across her palm and Lapis blood dripped down her arm and into the bowl. Lilliana was next. She gave me a small reassuring smile just before she pulled the blade through her hand, and her Gold blood dripped like tiny raindrops into the bowl.

The two men holding me pushed me forward. The one on my right took hold of my hand and held it out over the bowl.

"Please don't do this."

"Oh, stop your whining, it's just a small cut," Aaron snapped at me. "Be thankful we're kinder than our ancestors. They would have slaughtered you as an offering."

"I'm begging you, please don't do this," I whispered as I tried to hold back tears.

"Well, well. It looks like there's something you're afraid of after all."

My abilities rushed to the surface, blurring my vision. I struggled to free myself once more when I felt the tip of the blade dig into my arm and slice my skin.

Silver blood poured from me into the bowl. A gasp moved through the room, almost as if it was choreographed, and the blade Aaron had been holding hit the floor.

"What the fuck?" Aaron snarled, and the whole room plunged into darkness.

CHAPTER 25

The room erupted into chaos. Glass shattered and people screamed. As my eyes adjusted to the dark, I realized it wasn't an illusion. Someone had cut the power.

I started to sneak across the stage, trying to make an escape, when a pair of arms wrapped around me and took me down to the ground. I landed hard on my shoulder and pain shot down my body like a lightning bolt.

"You're not going anywhere," Aaron growled. "I knew there was something wrong with you." He was on top of me, pinning me to the floor as he held the dagger at my throat.

"Are you a spy? Who sent you?" Aaron snapped and the edge of the blade slipped. A trickle of blood dripped down the side of my neck and I had to fight to control my breathing.

"What are you talking about? Sent me? I was *Chosen*," I

reminded him. "Who would have sent me? The Silvers haven't been seen in generations."

The few that survived the slaughter scattered, never to be seen again, according to my mother.

"Don't lie to me!" I could feel him shaking with rage above me and though I could only make out the outline of him, I knew he was moments from pulling the blade across my neck.

"I don't know what you're talking about." Hot angry tears stung my eyes. I refused to die like an animal. Summoning up my strength, I let my abilities free. No point in hiding who I was anymore. I bucked my hips as the electric current of my abilities sizzled over my skin. Aaron convulsed and I hit him square in the face. He tumbled to the side, and I pushed him off of me.

"Bitch," Aaron snarled.

I stumbled to my feet, cursing the dress for getting tangled up in my legs.

I started to make a run for it when I was yanked backward and twisted around. Aaron stood behind me, his shoe on the satin fabric of my dress. He leveled his eyes on me and wiped the blood from his face.

"I'm going to enjoy gutting you," he seethed.

"I'd like to see you try." Instead of trying to run away from him, I charged him. A split second of shock crossed his face before I knocked directly into him. An illusion started to pull at the corner of my vision, and I summoned my abilities. I wasn't going to let him suck me into another of his tortures.

I let my rage guide my abilities as pure, raw energy

crawled down my exposed skin and latched onto Aaron. The dagger fell from his hand and a slow smile spread across my lips.

As I reached to grab the dagger, someone grabbed my arm. The electricity coursing through me should have knocked them on their ass, but they didn't flinch.

Looking to my left, Jayce's eyes met mine. I watched as Jayce eyed me carefully, not making a move. He knew what I was now. I could feel my Silver blood trailing down my arm. I felt no fear anymore as I let in the darkness, ever so slowly.

Taking a step towards Jayce, the ambiance around me fell away as I gave into instinct. I knew what I had to do. I didn't think. With a swift swipe of my arm, I attempted to punch him, but he caught my fist and twisted my hand to the side, and pulled me against his body.

"I'm trying to help you," he whispered into my ear.

I wasn't stupid enough to believe him. I stomped on his foot, but instead of letting me go his grip tighten on me.

"Let go of me," I yelled into his chest.

His grip loosened on me and he allowed me to take a step back.

"If you want to live to see another day, we have to get out of here."

I shook my head and started to back away.

"Now, Willow," he yelled. I was so stunned that he'd called me by my first name and not Ms. Knight that I didn't put up a fight when he started to pull me away from the stage and toward the service stairwell.

There were people everywhere, pushing and shoving their way around the darkness. Glass cracked under my shoes as Jayce pulled me behind him. Someone yanked on my other arm and the gash in my arm screamed in pain.

"You're not going anywhere, filthy Silver," the man holding me practically growled.

I let go of Jayce's hand and turned on the spot. I wanted to kick at the person who had grabbed onto me, but this damn dress made that impossible.

With my free hand, I punched the guy in the face and his grip loosened on me. Grabbing his shoulders, I shoved my knees up into his groin and he double over.

Another hand grabbed my arm from behind and I whirled around, my fists searching for their next target. I connected with Jayce's face and he winced at the pain.

"Remind me not to get on your bad side," he smirked.

"Who said you were on my good side?"

He shook his head, and we continued pushing through the crowd. Punching in a code on the door, it clicked open, and he shoved me onto the landing. Slamming the door behind him, he elbowed the data pad on this side of the door and the screen shattered.

"That should buy us a minute," he said slightly out of breath. "Come here." He stepped toward me and motioned for me to give him my arm.

"I don't need or want your protection. I can handle myself." My voice was low and careful. I tried to keep my anger down, but it was a hard thing to accomplish.

"I know, Willow." His voice was surprisingly soft and genuine.

I hesitated, not sure if I could trust him. Yes, he had gotten me out of immediate danger, but why? What was his angle?

He closed the distance between us and dropped to his knee. Grabbing hold of my dress, he ripped a strip of the fabric off of the bottom. Getting back to his feet, he grabbed my arm and wrapped the satin around the gash.

"We don't need you leaving a trail of blood." He tied off the fabric and let go of my arm.

"Thanks," I said, unsure of what to feel.

"We need to keep moving." He started down the stairs. "That door won't hold for much longer." As the words left his mouth a loud bang against the door shattered the silence.

I pulled my dress up to my knees and bolted down the stairs. This was why I hated wearing dresses, they were so impractical when it came to running and fighting. I didn't look back to see if Jayce was following me and really, I didn't care. It was my life on the line, my blood that had been spilled for everyone to see.

As I reached the fourth floor landing, I was about to continue down the stairs when Jayce grabbed me and hauled me through the door.

"This way."

"Why are you helping me?" I asked as I followed him down the hall.

"There will be plenty of time for questions later. Let's get you somewhere safe first." He pushed through a door into one of the small guest rooms I'd put together over the last week. There was already someone inside.

"Jax, I need your help."

Jaxtyn turned to look at us and his eyes darted to the dried silver blood all over my arm.

"By the Gods," he said under his breath. "Are you alright?" He crossed the room and reached for my arm gently. "How the hell did this happen?"

"Fucking Aaron and his Blood Ritual," Jayce looked like he wanted to punch a hole through the wall.

"I'll take care of her." Jaxtyn gripped Jayce's shoulder. "Get back up there before someone notices you're missing. We'll meet you at the tavern."

"Wait, where are we going?" I looked between the two of them, but they ignored me.

"If I'm not there by sunrise, leave without me and get her to the safe house."

"You'll be there." Jaxtyn nodded once to Jayce.

"Willow, I need you to go with Jax. He'll keep you safe."

"I don't understand what's happening. Neither of you seem surprised that I have Silver blood." I looked between the two of them and they shared a secretive glance.

Jayce placed his hands on my shoulder and his eyes met mine. "That's because we already knew."

"How?" My brow furrowed as I searched his eyes.

"I'll explain everything, I promise. I just need you to trust us right now." He put his hand on my cheek as he said this, and looked me in the eye for a few seconds. Then, he looked back to Jaxtyn.

"We *are* trying to keep you alive, after all," Jaxtyn raised his eyebrows and smiled.

"I don't need your help getting me out of the house," I said letting my abilities course through me.

"Willow, be..." Jayce trailed off as I started to vanish right before their eyes.

"Well, that makes things easier," Jaxtyn chuckled.

Jayce looked back at me, though he couldn't see me anymore. "Be careful." He nodded once and left the room.

"You too," I said but the door had already closed.

CHAPTER 26

"Okay. This is weird," Jaxtyn said, but he was wearing a grin that told me he was absolutely loving it. What a lunatic.

"I'm still here. If you just walk out through the front doors and don't let them slam too quickly behind you, I can follow with no problem," I said as his eyes scanned the room trying to find the source of my voice.

With a quick nod, Jaxtyn turned to leave. As we peeked out of the door, chaos surrounded us.

"Shit," he muttered, turning his head side to side and surveying the scene around us. People were running back and forth, looking worried, angry, or suspicious. They were ducking into every room, checking under beds, tearing apart closets, and rummaging through bathrooms. The hallways were packed, and sneaking through while invisible was going to be tricky.

"I'll meet you at the front door," I whispered as I tried

to slip past Jaxtyn. We would move quicker if I could maneuver around myself and not have to worry about him. I brushed past him and he threw his arms out to catch me, reaching into thin air and finding a solid body right in front of him.

"Willow, we stay together. That's what Jayce told us to do. He would absolutely kill me if you got caught."

"Fine," I whispered, "but we can't go this way. I won't be able to dodge this many people."

"Okay. Let's just think about this for a minute. Is there a back way, a…a…servant's door or something?"

"Don't you think that would be the first place they're going to look, considering I'm a servant?"

Jaxtyn looked sheepish, shrugging his shoulders and looking around.

"Could we climb over the garden wall?"

"*I* could," I answered, "But if anyone saw you climbing over the wall, they'd get a bit suspicious, don't you think?"

Jaxtyn closed his eyes and took a deep breath. "Okay. We can't get out the front way, there's too many people. We can't use the servant's entrance, because there's bound to be guards there. And no climbing over the wall, because you might get out, but I'd probably be captured, or at least followed. We have no options."

"We have an option. You can walk out the front door, and I can-"

"No options that I'm willing to take." Jaxtyn interrupted me.

He was starting to really annoy me. The obvious choice was to separate, and regroup later. The longer we stood here peering out the door, the more chance he had of getting caught. As usual, it would just be easier to work alone. *Think, Willow!*

"Jayce would want us to-" Jaxtyn began.

"What difference does it make what Jayce wants? He's not here! He left us to figure it out on our own!" I said angrily. I didn't realize until I said it that I was mad at him for leaving me. I knew he trusted Jaxtyn, and that both of them knew my secret, but it should be Jayce here with me, helping me. It was his house. He knew all its secrets and passageways. We wouldn't be having this problem if he had just stayed.

"Jayce had to leave, you know that. It would have been too dangerous for him to not help his brother search for you. And we need him throwing them off our scent. He'll find us at the safe house."

"I don't need him to throw off my scent. I'm invisible, remember? I just need someone to open the door for me."

"You don't have to do this alone anymore, Willow! I know you've been hiding who you are your whole life, but we've got you. We need to stick together so I can show you the way to the safehouse and we can get you out of this region. Your invisibility is a huge asset, but it's not the only thing you need."

I started to disagree with him, but stopped myself. Sure, I had been doing fine on my own for the most part, keeping my head down and hiding my blood. But obviously I hadn't done a great job, because Jayce had known. He had most likely Chosen me only because I was a Silver, and he had known it from the very beginning. *What was going on?*

I peeked out the door again, trying to find a way to weave through the crowds. I was invisible, but still solid. If someone bumped into thin air, they would know what had just happened. It wasn't like Silver abilities were a secret.

"Ok, Jaxtyn. Let's just walk out this door. Try and go slowly, I'm going to stay close on your heels, and try to avoid touching anyone else. I'll keep a hand on your shoulder so you know I'm there, and we won't have a problem."

Gods, me and my big mouth. We made it down the hall and Jaxtyn moved towards the elevator. I froze.

"No!"

"Willow, no one is going to believe I'm not up to something if I take the stairs. You're like, the only person in the region that actually uses them."

I refused to admit to Jaxtyn that I was afraid, but my nerves were so frazzled with the stress of being discovered as a Silver that I didn't think I could hold it together.

"It's too small. If a few other people come in, they'll for sure step on me or bump into me." Good, a perfect excuse. "Just say you're looking for me if someone catches you in the stairwell."

"Fine," Jaxtyn said, clearly getting annoyed at me. "You do realize *I'm* supposed to be the one saving *you*, right?"

There was no one in the stairwell. Even in a panic, Mystics refused to exert any extra energy. Unbelievable.

When we stepped out of the stairwell and into the main entrance, we ran into another problem. There were guards to the door, and a crowd gathered. They were checking everyone, slowly letting them trickly out one by one. It would be too risky to sneak out behind Jaxtyn. The doors were closing basically on people's heels to stop anyone else from sneaking through.

"Ok," Jaxtyn said, quickly analyzing the situation. "What if we went and hung out in the simulation for a bit. When they come looking, they'll just find me in my usual spot, right? I'm always there helping Jayce out," Jaxtyn said, throwing out another idea.

Not recently, I thought. Jayce had asked me to join him in the simulation room to help him out, pretending it was to give Jaxtyn a night off. Now I know it's because he was trying to see if I slipped up and let my abilities loose while under the pressure of the simulation. I had been used, and it really pissed me off. Thank the Gods I had stopped doing that. I was almost grateful that Aaron kept me too busy to get there. Other than the last time, when the simulation went wrong, Jayce hadn't even tried to have me join him in a few weeks, since that fight we had in the…

"Basement!" How could I have forgotten! I grabbed Jaxtyn and pushed him back into the stairwell. "Take us down to the basement, I know the way out."

To his credit, Jaxtyn followed my orders without comment, trusting me to get us out of the house. I didn't know what I had done to earn that trust, but thank the Gods I had it. Jaxtyn maneuvered through the stairwell looking calm and almost bored. He moved slowly, like he didn't have a care in the world, putting on a front in case we ran into any more people.

It felt so good to use my abilities. It had been a while since I could hold my invisibility for this long, and my skin practically hummed with power. And having two people who knew what I was, and were still willing to help me, felt *good.* I knew I should be suspicious, but I trusted Jayce. What would the point of all of this be, if he was going to just hand me over to the authorities?

We reached the basement without incident, and then things became more difficult. Jaxtyn had no reason, really, to be down here, and as we finally reached the basement door, Jaxtyn slammed into a guard on his way up.

"What are you doing down here?" the guard asked. Behind him I could see a few more guards heading up the stairway. I was helpless, and could only watch and hope that they didn't take Jaxtyn away. I shouldn't have worried, though. Jaxtyn was always such a sweet talker.

"Jayce asked me to help him look for the servant girl who's gone missing," he said without hesitation.

"She's not a servant. She's a Silver," the guard said with venom.

"Is she?" Jaxtyn asked, sounding bored. "That's the rumor I heard, but I didn't see the ceremony."

"Where were you?"

"What's it to you where I was?" My body was tense as I watched. Jaxtyn's tone was defensive, and the guard instantly suspected something was up with him.

"Someone shut off the lights just as the Silver was

revealed, helping her escape. So I'll ask again, *sir,* where were you?" the guard said, clearly losing patience.

"Goodness, that was done on purpose? Maybe I'll help you come find them instead of looking for the servant girl. I was getting friendly with a gorgeous blond Gold when they went out. She got scared and ran off, and with all this chaos I'll never find her again," Jaxtyn answered. He put a pained look on his face. "I was so close. If she hadn't had all those buttons on that dress..."

"Oh man, don't even get me started," the guard laughed. "We already checked the basement, but you're free to take another look."

Gods, men were so dumb.

He stepped out of the basement and Jaxtyn moved to the side to let him and his fellow guards through. When they had turned the corner and were out of sight, both of us let out a huge sigh of relief.

"Ok, Willow. What next?"

I let go of my invisibility and raced down the stairs, trying to remember which wall of boxes was hiding the way out. Finally, I found it, and we started moving the boxes carefully to the side. It was slow work. We had to be sure no one was listening, and we had no idea if anyone was waiting on the other side of the archway. After what felt like hours, the stone archway was visible at the top of the stack now, with just enough space for both Jaxtyn and I to squeeze through. We'd have to leave it open once we got through, but there was no reason for anyone to think I had help escaping through this. I thanked the Gods for red curtains as I turned to Jaxtyn.

"Jaxtyn, I have to go through first," I said, and cut him off when he began to argue. "What are you going to say if you crawl through here and run directly into a guard. Or Aaron? I can get out and keep watch, so that we know it's all clear for you to climb out."

"Okay. I don't like it, but it does make sense. Where does this doorway lead?"

"Good question."

"You don't *know*?"

"How am I supposed to know? It reaches outside. Shouldn't that be enough?"

Jaxtyn put his head in his hands for a second, and sighed.

"Okay. Climb out, and then *don't move.* You understand?"

"Jaxtyn, I'll be invisible, I can sneak around and make sure there's no one there. I'm not helpless!"

"Just climb out, Willow. Take a *quick* look and give me an ok."

I slipped back into my invisibility and climbed up the stack of boxes and out of the opening at the top. I had to fight my way through a few bushes, branches catching on my dress and tearing the beautiful fabric. When I finally emerged from the bushes, I was facing more trees, darkness, and not much else. The night air was cool, and the sky was clear. The moon was shining brightly, which would make it more difficult for Jaxtyn to slip away. I peered around, straining to hear any footsteps or voices, but it was silent. I couldn't tell what part of the house I had just exited. In the night, it all looked the same. I couldn't even see the garden wall.

"All clear, Jaxtyn!"

I could hear him scrambling up behind me, fighting his way through the thick bushes, and when he emerged, he looked around and laughed. The noise startled me, ringing through the quiet night.

"Are you insane?" I asked, putting my hands over his mouth.

"Willow, do you know where we are?"

"Obviously not," I said, losing patience.

"We're outside the house. Outside the garden walls. We turn that corner and the road to lead us to the village is right there! You did it!"

"We still have to get to the safehouse."

"Yeah, but if you stay invisible, I'm just another person strolling along the street finding my way home after the party. There's no reason for them to suspect me- I'm Jayce's best friend! Ha! You're a genius! I don't think even Jayce knows this is here!"

I looked around again and realized why I hadn't recognized what part of the house I was in. We had emerged from the side of the house, through the thick hedge that surrounded the garden wall to give the Starrs more privacy. Looking back at where we came, I couldn't see the stone archway at all. It was completely hidden by the thick bushes, and if you didn't know it was there, it would have been impossible to find. A true secret exit. A shame we couldn't replace the stack of boxes to cover it back up. Once they found out how I'd escaped, they'd probably have it closed over to stop that from ever happening again. *Jayce, I hope you find those misplaced boxes first.*

"We have Aaron to thank for that," I said with a little laugh.

Jaxtyn reached out to give me a hug in his excitement, but caught nothing but air, and starting giggling all over again. I couldn't help but laugh along with him softly as we walked into the night to freedom.

CHAPTER 27

I stood at a window, watching the sky shift from black to baby blue. I was exhausted- I hadn't slept a wink last night. I was too wired after our escape from the Starr residence to sleep.

I was only half surprised when Jaxtyn led me into town and straight to the alley I'd seen Jayce sneak down when I first got here. Once we got inside, I was given a fresh, albeit old, set of clothes to change into, and I immediately felt more like myself than I had since the Choosing ceremony.

I'd been curious about what was inside the secret door in the alleyway since I first saw it, but I had to admit, I was pretty disappointed. The entire place was the size of my bedroom back at the Starr house, and it was dark and grimy. Not that I was expecting anything lavish, but I'd thought it would be a little more exciting since it was worth hiding behind an illusion. I came to find out that it was the people who came through here who are worth hiding, not the place itself.

I'd tried to sleep when we first arrived. Using my abilities to that extent had taken their toll, and I desperately needed rest. There were a few cots along the walls that were comfortable enough, but no matter how long I lay there, I couldn't fall asleep. The whole night kept flashing through my mind. Silver blood, the anger in Aaron's eyes. The fact that he thought someone sent me to spy on him. I'd wondered where that thought came from. But Jayce was the most confusing of all. He'd helped me escape, and he'd already known about my blood. Had known all along, in fact. Had specifically had me Chosen because of it, and then never said a word once I arrived. After a while, I gave up on sleep and decided to keep watch, looking out of the window for any sign of trouble.

Jayce still hadn't made it to the small tavern the illusion from the alleyway hid, and I was starting to think he never would.

"It's dawn. Are you ready to go, Willow?" Jaxtyn asked.

I nodded and turned away from the window.

Jayce stood in the doorway with Jaxtyn, and my whole body reacted to seeing him.

"You made it." The words were barely a whisper on my lips.

"And just in time." Jaxtyn clapped a hand on his shoulder.

Jayce shrugged and closed the door behind him. "We're going to need you to go invisible again," Jayce met my eyes. "Do you think you can hold on until we're safely out of town?"

"Yes, but I can't leave yet."

"Ms. Knight, we don't have time to go back and forth. It's now or never." The fact that he was back to calling me Ms. Knight did not go unnoticed. I ignored it. This was too important.

"I won't leave my brother. Not again. I just got him back."

"Your brother?" Jayce's brow furrowed.

"He's who I was looking for when you caught me sneaking out. He's a Scarlet."

"And here I thought you hated all Mystics."

"There are a few exceptions." I folded my arms across my chest.

"A few, huh?"

"Don't get your hopes up, you're not on the list." I leveled my eyes on him.

"Am I?" I heard Jaxtyn ask quietly. Jayce ignored him.

"Not even after I saved your life?" He smirked.

I just stared at him, unwilling to take another step until he agreed to find Eli.

"Fine." He turned to Jaxtyn. "Can you look for..." he turned back to me.

"Elias Knight, he knows Lilliana. She was at the Gala last night- a Gold."

"Well, you certainly do have surprising friends. Lilliana's one of us. I'll grab her and we'll see what I can do, but on one condition," Jaxtyn looked at me. "You leave now with Jayce and I'll follow once I've got your brother."

I opened my mouth to argue.

"Nope," he held up his hand to silence me. "That's the deal. Take it or leave it."

"And if I say no?" I cocked my head to the side and looked between the two of them.

"We don't need you conscious," Jayce answered. "You'll be leaving here in the next couple minutes no matter your answer."

"Back to threats," I scoffed.

"It's not a threat." Jayce stepped toward me and his eyes bore into mine.

I opened my mouth to respond, but nothing came out. I nodded once instead.

"See you at the safe house." Jaxtyn gripped Jayce's shoulder. "Take care, Willow, and try not to do anything stupid." He winked and headed out the door.

"When you're ready," Jayce pointed toward me and motioned up and down.

Understanding his meaning, I summoned my abilities, and the invisibility crept down my arms, legs, and torso until I was completely hidden in plain sight.

"Hold onto my arm." He tapped the back of his arm. "We're going to be moving fast. Whatever you do, don't let go."

I nodded and quickly realized he couldn't see me. "Fine, let's just get this over with."

He opened the door and we stepped into the alley. Soft morning light kissed our skin as we made our way onto one of the main streets. Without warning, he turned left and we were smack dab in the middle of a market. There were people everywhere, buying fresh fruits and vegetables, as well as small handmade trinkets.

At first, I wondered how we were going to make it through the crowd without bumping into everyone as we went, but of course, I'd forgotten that most people were afraid of Jayce. He must have looked fiercer and angrier than normal, because people jumped out of the way when they saw him.

Before I knew it we were turning toward the port where I'd arrived.

"We're taking a ship? Are you nuts?" I said under my breath.

"I am supposed to be looking for you, and what better way to do a search of the area? We're going to take it a short ride away, and then rough it on foot the rest of the trip. They can track the ship, but if we're careful enough they can't track us after we leave it. I just have one stop to make first, a quick meeting." I could hear the humor in his voice. As much as I wanted out of here, I wasn't sure how I felt about getting onto a ship again.

As we approached the gate, several guards stopped us before we could move any further.

"Mr. Starr." One of the guards tried for a smile, but it came off more like a grimace. "How can we help you?"

"I'm sure you've heard we're searching for a girl," he started.

"A Silver, I heard. Better to kill her right away before she tries to take over any of these regions." One of the other men spoke and Jayce's head snapped in his direction. "I mean, sorry, umm… yes we heard," the man amended.

"Yes well, I need a ship so I can search the area."

"Yes of course." The first guard who spoke to Jayce motioned him forward.

My grip tightened on his arm as I slipped past the other guards unnoticed.

We were taken to a ship, and the guard helped Jayce get everything ready for takeoff while I hid in the back against the wall. This ship was much smaller than the last one I'd been on. There were only two seats up at the front and the rest of the ship was nothing more than an empty metal shell.

"Is there anything else?" The Guard asked as he slowly started to back away towards the door. He clearly wanted out of here as quickly as possible. How Jayce made everyone around him so fearful of him, I'll never understand.

Jayce waved him off and started up the engine. The guard made his exit and slammed the door closed. I let out a sigh of relief and sunk down to the floor. The fact that we'd managed to get this far was a miracle. I was sure if anyone other than Jayce was trying to take a ship right now, they would have thrown them in prison for questioning.

Jayce got up and walked to the door, pulling on a lever to lock it into place. He turned toward the back of the ship and his eyes searched for me.

"I'm here." My voice sounded weak and small.

"Once we're in the air, you can come sit up front." He

turned back toward the front of the plane. "Until then, hold on." He took a seat and strapped in. I grabbed the netting that was hanging along the wall and held on with a death grip.

The engines roared to life and my stomach erupted with butterflies. Within seconds, we were in the air and I was pretty sure if I'd eaten anything in the last twelve hours, it would be all over the floor of the ship right now.

"Ms. Knight, it's safe to come up here now."

Breathe in through the nose, out through the mouth, I chanted to myself.

"Willow?" His voice held an edge of concern.

"I'm good here, thanks," I yelled to him.

He didn't try to convince me to join him and I went back to chanting with my face pressed against the cold metal wall. I closed my eyes and tried to focus on my breathing so I wouldn't think about the fact that we were flying unnaturally through the air.

At some point, I must have fallen asleep because I was jolted awake by the sound of thunder. Sitting upright, I noticed that my invisibility had faded and I was back to my solid self. From my position on the floor, I could just barely see out the front window. The sky had turned a dark grey while I'd slept and rain pelted the glass.

Thunder rolled overhead like the fury of the Gods. Lightning came as a brilliant shock of white. The constant barrage of it lit up the clouds, which were morphing and tumbling across the sky.

It made me think of my mom. She'd love watching storms from the front porch and always said, "*Why be afraid of darkness, when light always follows?"* She'd taught us to embrace and respect the strength of nature. That was easier said than done when you were flying through the storm.

Another flash of lightning filled the ship with light and I felt it start to descend.

"Umm, everything okay?" I croaked.

"We're a few minutes out from the meeting point if you want to come up," he replied, but somehow didn't answer my question.

"Is it safe?" I asked. "Won't I be seen?"

"Just trust me, Willow. We're making a quick stop, and no one will see you."

I got to my feet and slowly moved toward the front of the ship. I plopped down in the empty seat and stared out of the window. I couldn't see anything but rain and clouds, and immediately I regretting coming up here.

"You okay? You're looking a little green." His tone was half worried, half amused.

"I hate flying." I gripped the armrests, shut my eyes, and reminded myself to take deep breaths again.

"We'll be on the ground in a minute," he reassured me.

We landed with a thud, and I rushed out of the door the moment Jayce opened it, desperate to be back on solid ground. I didn't think I'd ever get used to flying. I didn't know where I was, but the scent reminded me of back home.

CHAPTER 28

It made me think of my dad, and my knees shook a bit. He would be so worried, and he might never know what happened to me. I wondered if I could convince Jayce to grab him from the village. I overheard Jayce mentioning us going to the Silver region. If there were other Silvers like me in the region, it seemed like the safest place for us to be. Surely the Silvers wouldn't mind a Commoner among them? They would understand more than anyone the fear and danger of being under the control of the other Mystics. The rain had started to let up by the time we landed, though the sky was still cloudy. I could hear crows crying in the distance, begging for food just like the rest of us. We must be close to some village where they could find some scraps. I wanted to be back home with my father, fighting over those scraps with those crows in the village square, dodging the others to get the best bits of food. My heart ached at the familiar thought. I missed home. Although I had to keep my distance from the rest of the village, they were kind to me, for the most part. The guilt I felt for stealing from them haunted me, but I knew what I had to do to keep my family alive.

Family was all I ever had growing up. I was too broken to make friends, and even if I wasn't, it would have been too dangerous. It wasn't easy to hide being a Silver. Losing my mom and brother ignited something dark in me that I never knew I had. My father used to call it an evil. Well, he called *me* evil. After it happened, he had blamed for my mom dying, and my brother getting sent away. It hurt, but I knew he didn't mean it, and as time passed, he stopped being so harsh. He was a drunk, and never remembered saying those things to me. I forgave him with each word that sliced at my heart, the knife of his tongue getting duller with each day. He lost the love of his life and a son. Besides, I was rightfully the one to blame in the first place, no matter how much Eli blamed himself.

Lost in memory, I could hear my fathers' deep voice. It always had a tone to it that made me feel like I was in trouble. Time felt like it slowed down as my name piqued my attention.

"Willow?" I *could* hear him. My eyes flew open in shock. Standing a short distance away, Jayce close behind him, was my father.

"Dad?" My voice shook. I was scared to move, afraid that it would all end up being an illusion. A cruel joke. Last time I saw him I was being pulled away to begin my time with the Starr family. I had been so worried about him. So scared that he wouldn't be able to take care of himself with me gone. I looked closely at him now as I walked to him. He didn't look much different, his eyes still red and watery, still too thin. But he was alive, and that was all that mattered. I ran and threw my arms around him, tears grazing my eyes.

"You're real! You're here, Dad!" I didn't want to let go. I couldn't believe it. It felt like ages since I had seen him last. I hadn't realized how much I had been worrying about him until seeing him alive and well released a tension I didn't know I was holding.

"Why … how are you here? What's going on?"

"I'm real, Willow. But this is dangerous. You shouldn't be here!" he chastised. I pulled back, meeting his dark gaze. He was crying, but he looked angry as well.

"What do you mean?" My heart sank. I wasn't sure what I'd expected. Maybe a smile? A warm hello? He was so nice to me the last time I saw him. Sober, and affectionate. I thought things had turned around for him. This wasn't the reaction I wanted. He was wearing a frown, and worry spread across his face as he eyed Jayce and the ship.

"They're looking for you, Willow. They already came to the house and tore it apart, like the night…." Oh, no. My poor father had to relive it all again. I hope they were at least gentle with him. It was a miracle he was alive, and an even bigger miracle that he was currently sober.

"You need to get out of here. I don't know where they are but I doubt they would leave the area just yet. It's not safe for any of us! They said they'd burn the whole village down if they found you here!" He pushed me towards the tree line to get some cover, so we weren't standing in the open.

"Jayce has a meeting here –"

Jayce cleared his throat. "Ah, that wasn't exactly true. It was just a little lie to get you here, as a surprise. I knew how badly you wanted to see your father again. I wanted you to know he was safe."

"Are you stupid, boy?" My father was wide eyed, and I couldn't believe he'd just spoken to a Mystic like that. I never saw him so flustered and sober at the same time. Usually when he hadn't had anything to drink, he was a lot more patient and focused, but his eyes were darting in every direction and his breathing was quick and uneven. I was trying to figure out what was wrong with him, thinking maybe he was sick, but then it hit me. He was absolutely terrified.

Jayce opened his mouth to respond, but closed it quickly, looking confused. He didn't know how to react to my father. I don't know if anyone but me had spoken to him like that before. I don't think I'd ever seen him speechless. It would have made me laugh if I wasn't so worried about my dad.

"Jayce can keep us safe, he's part of the Scarlet leadership. If they see us, he can tell them he caught us and are bringing us back, and they'll leave us alone. You can relax a little, Dad."

"Who said it was the Scarlets I was afraid of? Willow, please, just listen to me. There are people…things you couldn't even dream of. You need to keep your head down and stay safe. And stay away from here! I'm trying to keep you safe, darling." His eyes softened as he finished, finally focusing on me fully. "Look at you. You haven't been gone long, but you did a lot of growing up. I'm proud of you, and seeing you now is a gift. But you need to leave quickly, before we're seen. I'm not sure what they'll do…"

"What who will do, Mr. Knight?" Jayce asked, interrupting. It was a good question. If it wasn't the Scarlets, who was looking for me?

"I…I cannot. Even speaking of them is dangerous. I will try to keep them at bay for as long as I can, but eventually they'll find you. Willow, promise me. Promise me you won't fight them. You can't win! You don't know what you're up against! You need to try to stay safe. I am sorry that you don't understand now, but you will later on. Please, leave," he urged.

I glanced at Jayce, but he was as clueless as I was. I felt uneasy. Was this real? Or had years of abusing his body with alcohol finally taken its toll on my father?

"Dad, why don't you come with us?" I asked. Jayce turned to look at me sharply, but I didn't care. I couldn't leave him like this, not in this state. It was worse than finding him passed out drunk in our house.

"I don't belong with you, Willow. Not yet."

"But Dad, I found Eli! We could be a family again! And we could be safe! We'll run away, and no one will ever find us."

My father sighed a deep, bone-weary sigh. "They will always find us, Willow."

He was starting to creep me out a little bit. I was

getting an uneasy feeling, a prickling on the back of my neck like someone was watching me. I glanced at Jayce and saw him frowning, obviously a little shaken by my father's words too. I nodded at him, and he stepped forward.

"Mr. Knight, we have to go. I'm sorry we can't stay longer. I don't know how much help I can offer, but if you need anything, come to this clearing. There's a small house on the other side, a few steps into the forest. I'll have my people check there once a week. Leave us a note, or just hide out there, and we'll assist you in any way you can."

My father looked at Jayce with sad eyes. "My boy, there are things even Mystics cannot help me with. Take my daughter to safety, and watch over her."

"I will guard her with my life, Mr. Knight." Wow. *Talk about dramatic, Jayce.*

"Dad, are you sure you don't want to come with us?"

"My dear, your mother was always the brave one, not me. I'm just glad you inherited her courage, and not my weakness. Go, and be safe. Tell Eli I love him." He hugged me as tightly as he could, and then turned and walked back towards the village. Tears were streaming down my face as I realized this would probably be the last time I ever saw him.

"Willow," Jayce said gently, "Let's get back on the ship. We still have a long way to go before we're safe."

I turned to him. "Something's not right here. Can't we check it out for a minute? I can turn invisible and..."

"I'll have someone else take a look. It's too dangerous

for us to be here. They can track the ship, remember? They think I'm out here looking for you, but the longer I linger, the more suspicious it gets."

I sighed. "Ok. Let's go back to the flying death trap."

I turned away from where my father had gone, and left him behind.

CHAPTER 29

Hours later, I was still stuck on the stupid ship. "Where are we exactly?" "We're about two hours south, on the way to the Silver region, just like we were the last time you asked. Once we land, we'll keep moving south." My eyes shot wide open and I stared at him. "The safe house is about hundred miles south of here, outside the reach of any region."

"But that's days away from the Scarlet region."

"It's only a couple hours by ship." He pushed a few buttons and the ship shuddered.

Fear punctured through me like a knife, and I closed my eyes again and braced for impact. The engines made a loud wheezing sound and we tipped from side to side until we hit something solid. Jayce flipped another few switches and the engines powered down.

We were on the ground, thank the Gods.

I opened my eyes and looked out the window. We were

surrounded by trees, and there was a heavy mist that clung to the air, making visibility horrible.

"We have about a ten-minute walk." Jayce pointed straight ahead. "Then we can rest." He got up from his seat and made his way toward the back. Opening the door, a burst of cold air rushed into the ship.

I turned in my seat so I could see him. "You said you'd answer my questions."

"And I will," he smiled and nodded for me to follow him.

I let out a heavy sigh. "Okay." Walking toward the door I hesitated. "Should I?" I motioned to myself and the fact that I was visible.

He shook his head and held out his hand. "You don't need to hide anymore, Willow."

My heart did a little flip at the sound of my name and I took his hand as he helped me jump down. He closed up the ship and we started through the forest. The noise of crunching leaves, twigs snapping, and the soft pitter-patter of rain on the canopy above us was the only sound as we walked.

After a few minutes of taking in my surroundings and shaking off my nervous stomach, I was finally ready to have my questions answered.

"Okay," I let out a huff of breath. "You said that you knew I was a Silver. How?"

The corner of his lips pulled into a smirk, but he kept his eyes straight forward. "Searching for Silvers is what I do," he started. "I got word that there was a Silver in your village, and so I poked around a bit." He looked at me then. "It was easy enough to find out your mother paid to have you branded as a Commoner."

"If it was easy, wouldn't others have found out before you?"

He shook his head before I even finished my sentence. "It's easy if you know where to look," he said with a satisfied expression. "The necklace you wear is a calling card for those who help hide, protect, and preserve the old way of life."

"What do you mean?" I shivered as the cold started to seep into my bones.

"There's a whole network of people who use that symbol to escape the current system," he nodded toward the necklace under my shirt. "They help Mystics who don't believe in being separate, and want to live free of tyrannical rule. They help Mystics who fall in love with Commoners, or Silvers who need to hide who they truly are." His eyes met mine and there was a sadness in them that cut deep.

"So through this network you found me, and that's why you had me Chosen?"

He nodded. "I was trying to help," he let out a heavy sigh. "But you were much more than I bargained for. It was always my plan to get you out of the Scarlet region and bring you here. It took a little longer to make the arrangements, and my brother's little ceremony certainly didn't help."

"But why do you even care?"

He paused on the path a few feet away from a cabin that was still partially hidden in the fog.

"I have many reasons," he shrugged. "I don't believe in treating Commoners the way Mystics do. I don't think the regions should be separate. People should be free to live how they want, Mystic and Commoner alike. But also... because of this."

He held out his hand, palm up between us, and pulled a dagger from his hip. Digging the tip of the blade into the middle of his palm, fresh Silver blood sprung up from the wound.

"You're... you're a Silver?" I gasped.

His eyes met mine, and for the first time I understood why he trained so hard. Why he made people fear him. He was just like me, and trying very hard to hide in plain sight.

"I've never met another Silver before," I said in disbelief. "I didn't even know any others existed."

He smiled and pointed toward the cabin. "Ready to meet some more?"

My eyes widened and my heart hammered in my chest. "Absolutely."

"Come on, let's get settled in. We have to wait a bit for Alexander to show up. Might as well get comfortable."

Inside the cabin was sparse. A couch and some chairs filled the main room, and I could see a small kitchen further to the back of the place. There was a fireplace and some logs waiting to be thrown in.

"I'll get the fire going. Check the kitchen- there should be some food. This is an active safe house."

"Jayce, you can't just say something like that and then expect me to not ask questions."

"Just go get us some food, Willow. I promise I'll answer your questions as soon as I can."

I stepped into the kitchen and started looking around for food. Jayce was right. It was stocked with essentials. In fact, it was a little overstocked. As I opened up one of the cabinets, and cup full of nails fell to the ground, making a loud crash.

"Sorry!" I yelled into the other room.

"Willow, this house has been used by our network for years. Try not to tear it down in your first few minutes here."

I stuck my tongue out in his direction, even though he couldn't see me. I would clean those up in a second. I was too hungry to do anything but eat.

I set up a tray of foods- breads, hard cheeses, and some dried meats, and spun around quickly. I felt my feet shoot out from under me as I slipped, falling towards the floor. I dropped the tray and flailed out my arms out to catch myself, but a pair of sturdy arms caught me before I touched the ground.

I gasped and looked up. I was face to face with beautiful cobalt eyes, wide and full of concern, and his pink, plump lips that were mouthing something to me.

"Hmm? What?" I blinked the world back into focus.

A knowing smirk covered his features. "I asked you if you were alright, Willow."

"Oh, yeah." Going against my body's wishes, I wiggled out of his grasp. As I lifted myself up, a sharp sting struck my foot. "Ouch."

"What happened?" Jayce quickly picked me back up.

"I must've cut it on one of the nails," I admitted sheepishly, glancing towards the mess I told myself I'd pick up after we ate.

"How did you survive this long without me?" He shook his head.

"I don't know, must be my limitless amount of luck." I began to twist myself around so that I could reach my foot, but Jayce had a tight grip on me. He held my foot straight, examining it. I began to grow tired as I was stuck resting back on my elbows. "Can I see it?"

"No."

"Well, how bad is it then?"

"Horrible."

I made a quick move to peek my head to the side so I could see just how horrible it was. I raised a brow at him, "Oh wow, it's just terrible. How will I ever survive such a cut?" On the side of my foot, a scratch was clearly displayed, a little bit of blood trailing down.

"A cut?" Jayce took his eyes off my foot for the first time, looking astounded. "It is a gash, nothing less. Let me fix it," he ordered. Deciding not to argue, I watched with amusement. Now that we were free of the Scarlet region, his walls were down, and he was...*silly*.

His brow was narrowed gravely. His hair was fell in a wave, golden streaks displayed from the sunlight peering through the window. His fingers touched my bare toes and I kicked with a jolt.

Squealing immediately, Jayce flinched. "That tickles!"

Narrowing his eyes at me, he said, "It's bleeding—can you stay still?" He tried to touch it again, and I rebounded in laughter which was immediately followed by uncontrollable kicking.

"Jayce. I can't," I pleaded, "it's…tickling…too much." My laughter continued with the kicking until he finally relented, releasing my foot.

"You're impossible," he rolled his eyes.

"Ummm….am I interrupting something?" an unfamiliar voice asked.

CHAPTER 30

Jayce jumped away from me, leaving me alone clutching my foot, my Silver blood on display. "You must be Willow! Thank the Gods Jayce got you out safely. I heard all about your big reveal at the Starr Gala." The strange man reached out and gave me a tight hug as if we were long lost relatives, not even reacting to my Silver blood.

"It's uh...nice to meet you. Who are you?"

"My name is Alexander, but my friends call me Xander. I'm one of the people in Jayce's network that keeps the Silvers safe."

"Are you a Silver too, Alexander?"

He winked at me and then blinked out of sight. I jumped. It was weird to see it from the other side. One second he was there, and then *poof,* no more Alexander. He appeared a few seconds later with a laugh.

"Your face! Have you never met another Silver?"

"Apparently I have," I said, giving Jayce a side glance, "but I didn't realize it."

"Xander," Jayce said, "The ship is a few miles north of here. Could you move it somewhere else for us, to keep them off our tails?"

"Will do, boss!" Alexander said with a little salute. "Willow, I'll see you at the safe house! Good luck!"

And with that he was out the door and moving quickly in the direction of the ship, leaving Jayce and I alone in the cabin.

"Get some rest, Willow. I'll keep watch and wake you when it's time to move. We could spare a few hours now that the ship is moving away from us."

For once, I listened, not having the energy to spar with him at that moment. I collapsed onto the couch, and within minutes had fallen into a deep sleep.

I was shaken awake what seemed like seconds later.

"Sorry, Willow, but we can't linger here too long. We've got to get moving if we want to make it to our next checkpoint."

"I'm not leaving here until I get some answers. You're a Silver! How is that even possible? There's just no way."

"Can we talk and walk? We really shouldn't linger."

I rolled my eyes. He always had to have his way, no matter what.

"Fine. Let's go," I said, walking past him and out the door. *Try and keep up, pretty boy.*

I heard Jayce chuckling behind me as we stepped into the wilderness.

"I guess I should start at the beginning," Jayce said as he

moved ahead of me to lead the way. "I know you had an education, but how much do you know about the Silver wars, and what things were like before that?"

"Um…"

"Not the greatest student, huh? Why am I not surprised."

I gave him a little shove, and he continued.

"Obviously you know how the Mystics were created. For thousands of years, all the regions lived together in harmony, including the Commoners. The Gods, for all their sibling rivalry, still respected each other, and wanted what was best for their children. Yes, they were jealous, especially Lethos, but when it came down to it, they were family. The Mystics should have been the same, able to intermingle and get along with each other. And they were, for a while. It used to be common for Mystics to marry other types of Mystics, or even Commoners."

"Jayce," I interrupted, "I don't need the history lesson. I've heard all this before. I'm more interested in the present."

"Are you never patient? My Gods, your teachers earned their pay with you. Anyway, so everyone was good for a long, long time. But then a few hundred years ago, there was a drought, and with no water, there were no crops able to grow on their own. It fell to the Verdants to help, and they did all they could. And as they worked themselves to exhaustion, the Golds helped heal them and keep them strong. The Lapis and the Scarlets worked together to protect the food stores with illusions and security. The Silvers helped transport the food to all corners of the world to make sure no one went hungry. Through all this, the Commoners really didn't have much to do except drain the resources that the Mystics worked so hard to provide.

"The Mystic leaders got together and decided that they couldn't treat the Commoners as equals anymore, since they didn't do their fair share. They made plans to cut their resources and limit their freedoms, so that the Mystics could control what was going in and out of the Commoner regions, to make sure their people had more than enough and didn't have to share with those who just took from them, and didn't give. The only leader who refused to go along with this plan was the Silver . In fact, the leader of the Silvers told his people what was happening, and they all moved to protect the Commoners. But the Silvers weren't really equipped to deal with violence, so in the end they were all either killed or scattered."

"Ok. So what I'm hearing is that the Silvers were the only Mystics who weren't complete shweeds." Interesting. This wasn't the story they taught us in school.

Jayce laughed. "Yeah, that's a good summary. So anyway, since we all used to intermingle, we still get Mystics born to Commoner families, and vice versa. Sometimes the blood comes out generations after the last Mystic relative. There's no way to predict it. We also get Scarlets born to Verdant families, Golds born to Lapis families, and so on. You obviously get my point, considering your brother is a Scarlet, and you're a Silver. So, the Silvers never died out. They hid, and kept being born into the world. But it's dangerous to have a Silver child, and for many Mystics, it's better to put that child to death than face the consequences of raising them in secret.

"My parents, for all their faults, believe in doing what's morally right, and killing an innocent babe is never going to be right. I was dropped on their doorstep by someone who knew how they felt about the practice of killing Silver babies. They never knew who my parents were, but they raised me as their own, and kept my secret. They helped me fit in with the Scarlets as best they could. But I can't abandon my people and live a cozy life while they are hunted down like animals, or forced to hide themselves in fear. So I started using my resources to rescue whoever I could find."

"So you started this network to save the Silvers?" I asked. How could I have misjudged him so badly? Everything he did, from his cruelty to his secrecy, was done to save and protect Silvers.

"No, I didn't. They found me, actually. I was clumsy when I started, and had too many close calls. They caught me at it because I jumped in and tried to save someone they had their eye on, and when they realized what I was doing, they approached me. I didn't have the experience they did, but I had the resources."

I had so many questions, but my brain was too foggy to focus on them. I had only slept a little while, and we were walking through tough terrain. There would be time for more questions later, I hoped. We spent a long time walking in silence, and I started to take in my surroundings more. I had been in forests back home, but as we went further and further south, closer to the Silver region, it grew wilder than I had ever seen it. Untouched by human hands, the trees grew taller, and wider. Some of them were so wide I thought it would take me a full minute to walk around the trunk. There were birds in the trees that I had never seen before, and although I couldn't see them, I could definitely hear animals scurrying around on the ground around us. It felt like I was in another world.

I thought about all I knew about the Silver region and what it looked like. It has always been described as a mystical place, with tall mountains and gorgeous valleys. There were animals there that we only heard about in fairytales. Would it really be like that? Could I find a place that magical, and be allowed to stay?

After several hours of walking, we came across another small cabin, and I could see smoke coming from the chimney. Maybe Alexander had gotten here already. I heard that back when they were strong, Silvers could travel in a blink. Could it be true?

"Finally," I heard Jayce mutter. I had to laugh as I looked at him. He was sweaty, and his hair was tangles, with tiny twigs sticking out. I had wanted to see what he looked like when he wasn't so perfectly groomed, and I got my wish. I think I liked him better this way.

He gave me a quick smile, and I got that feeling that he heard what I was thinking, before he lead me inside.

"Willow! Thank the Gods you're alright!"

CHAPTER 31

Eli was here. Eli was *here,* and we were both safe. I don't know how I could ever repay Jayce. I smiled at him over Eli's shoulder as my brother gave me a tight hug.

I saw Jaxtyn clap Jayce on the back, relieved to see his friend again, and then I saw Jayce give Lilliana a familiar hug, before she turned to me and have me a warm smile.

"Willow, I'm so glad you're safe. I didn't know what we were going to do when Aaron outed you in front of everyone."

"You're one of them!" I said, surprised. "Why didn't you say something when I first met you?"

"I didn't realize who you were! And when Eli introduced you as his sister, it hit me, but it was too late. Eli didn't know about my work with the Silvers, and it wasn't the right time, or the right place, to let him know."

"She's filled me in on the way here. I'm going to join

them, Willow. I'm going to help you, and anyone else like you."

Of course he was. As much as I wanted to keep him out of danger, it made perfect sense for him to join. As a detective, he would have access to people and information that could help the network, and could even play interference with other detectives to protect the Silvers they found before they were caught by the authorities. I thought of what Jayce said about having the resources to help. He had been an excellent recruit for the operation, and Eli was right up there too.

After we said our hellos, Jayce and I both took some much needed showers- regular, not automatic, I noticed- and then joined the group as they were hanging out by the fire. Although we weren't fully safe in the Silver region yet, we were far enough away from the Scarlet region to relax a little. For the first time in my life, I felt safe letting down some walls. We all made small talk, getting to know one another without the constraints of Mystic society breathing down our necks. After an hour or so, Lilliana turned to me and looked me straight in the eyes.

"So, Willow. Want to tell me about that vision you had at the Gala?"

Turning to face a wide-eyed Lilliana, I felt my mouth hang open. "Vision? That's what that was? Does that mean it was real?"

I had never had a vision before that moment, and I wasn't sure what they meant. She must've seen the confused look on my face as her mouth dropped open.

"You never had one before? Huh. You aren't twenty yet, are you?"

I had almost forgotten about my birthday. My abilities had been growing more and more rapidly as it approached. They would settle in once my birthday hit, but what that meant, I really didn't know. "It's just a couple of weeks away," I admitted. With everything else going on, it didn't cross my mind. Besides, birthdays were never important to me. It just made me think of another year without my mom and brother. Funny how things change. This year, it would be my father who missed my birthday. The thought of him alone crushed me, my heart ached as I held back the tears.

"Do you know what's going to happen once you hit twenty?" Jayce asked, his voice gentle. That tone was never good.

"Uh, I get a really great and expensive gift from you?"

"You want me to get you a present? I just saved your life! Isn't that enough?"

"I want something really shiny," I answered, trying and failing to keep a straight face. I was hoping that joking around would distract them, because I was afraid to know what was coming.

"Willow," Lilliana began, "You don't have to worry. Nothing scary happens. It's like your abilities snap into place. They'll become easier to grasp, and they'll reach their full strength. Usually Mystics have years of training, so they know what abilities will be there once they turn twenty. Hopefully we can work on it now that you're here, and see what we're working with."

"Snap into place? Is it going to hurt?"

Lilliana laughed. "No, I meant figuratively. They won't get stronger after you hit twenty. Right now, they're growing and changing. Can you feel them sometimes, moving around and expanding inside of you?"

I shivered as I thought of it. Of course I felt them, always there just below my skin.

"Interesting," Lilliana said, noticing my discomfort and understanding it. "How have you been dealing with them?"

"Dealing with them?" I laughed spitefully. I was angry. Angry that I didn't even know what I could do. Angry that I've had to run away from myself for my entire life. Now, I was so far behind. "I can't control them, Lilliana. And I fear them."

Her eyes grew soft and rounded as she smiled warmly at me. "That's what Jayce and the rest of the Silvers we saved are here for. You were neglected, and forced to hide who you really are. Lots of people who cross into the Silver region were the same when they arrived. We've been able to help so many of them, and through them, we know what Silvers are capable of. We've also read all the lore and books, so even if you have an ability that hasn't shown up yet in the others, we can help you," she insisted. Her tone was calming, and I couldn't help but trust her words. I never had a friend before, but maybe, just maybe... I could see her being one.

"I don't even know what else I'm capable of. The only one I use is my invisibility. But I didn't use it for anything grand, I just used it to steal food for me and my dad. I used my abilities minimally to survive, nothing more or less."

Lilliana grabbed my hands gently, and I felt a wonderful warmth go through my body.

"You did what you had to do to survive. None of the Silvers we save have had the freedom to use their abilities openly before we brought them to the region. But since getting there, they've shown us everything the Silvers could do, and it's incredible. *You're* incredible, Willow."

She was using some kind of healing power on me to make me calm, I realized, and a few days ago I would have recoiled, but Lilliana, and everyone else in the room, had risked everything to save me. She wasn't the monster I thought she was.

"I only know how to go invisible. I never knew I could do anything else. What else do you think I could learn?"

"What about telepathy? Maybe some telekinesis? Silver's gifts revolve around traveling, transporting, and those types of things." I shook my head. The thought of having more abilities scared me. I had been hiding for so long, that learning to do more felt wrong.

"I don't know. . ." Talking about it made me nervous as my stomach bunched up at the thought of even trying to use my abilities. I was taught to never show them, it was hard to change something that was engrained in me my whole life.

"Try it," her voice was soft, gentle, but persistent. She looked around the room. "Try opening that window from here. Just push it up with your mind. It's not too heavy, it would be a good place to start." The fear was eating away at my stomach at the thought. It made me think of my mom, my dad.

"I only ever do it when I need to," I strained. I know the intoxicating feeling it would bring me when I used my invisibility. I wouldn't want to stop if I explored what else I could do, and I wasn't ready, especially in front of other people. Lilliana watched me carefully before nodding, not pestering me further about it. But I found myself trying, despite my fear. I was curious about what else I was capable of. I focused on the window, watching the firelight reflect in the glass. *Move,* I told it, feeling ridiculous even though no one could hear me. Nothing happened, but I kept pushing. Finally, I thought I saw a little wobble.

Before we could continue, I heard one quick knock sound on the door. My stomach dropped. My breathing hitched. My eyes grew wide as I stared at the door in anticipation. My abilities were suddenly in my clutches, as much as I tried to keep them at bay. When I saw the door begin to creak open, I took a step back, my heart racing. Next to me I heard a high-pitched clinking sound as glass shattered across the floor. My self-control was still a work in progress. Xander strode into the room, back from dropping Jayce's ship off somewhere else. "Are you okay?" He asked, looking at me with concern.

I opened my mouth to speak, trying to shake off the past memory. The night my mother died and my brother was taken away was constantly in the back of my mind. The simple knocking on the door brought back the fear and anger of that day, especially when I was in a room full of Mystics. Taking a deep breath, I closed my eyes for a moment, trying to remember that my brother was here for me. We were reunited again, and we were safe. The memory was just that- a memory.

"Willow? You're bleeding," Jayce whispered. My eyes shot open, and I could feel the sharp sting in my ankle, a glass shard from the window I had just broken stuck inside.

He rushed to me, but I quickly turned away. In a swift motion I bent down and tore it out, the silver blood oozing out slowly. "I'm fine, just a small cut," I rushed, pushing him away.

"You broke the window, Willow," Lilliana said, and for some reason she was smiling. "Now we know telekinesis is part of your powers. We just have to learn how to control it a little better." That last part was said with a hint of humor, and I laughed. A loud, genuine laugh. It felt so good to use my powers out in the open and not be judged for them, even if I was breaking stuff with it.

Lilliana reached towards me with her hands out, and before I could react, she had healed the cut on my ankle. My brother brought me a cloth to wipe away the blood as my heart stopped racing.

"Everything good, Xander?" Jayce asked.

"Of course it is! This is me you're talking about, Jayce. You might get all the credit, but I'm the brains behind this operation," Xander answered, plopping into a chair by the fire and giving me a ridiculous wink.

"We should all get some sleep, then. We leave at dawn."

CHAPTER 32

I think Jayce and I were the only ones who had no trouble waking up with the sun. When the morning arrived, our group set out from the cabin looking like a bunch of sleepwalkers. Bleary eyed and yawning, Eli, Jaxtyn, Lilliana, and Xander took forever to get packed and ready to go. Jayce and I waited outside, our eyes scanning the area for any signs of trouble. We should be safe, but you can never be too careful.

"How are you handling all this?" Jayce asked me.

I looked around the wild forest, with its enormous trees and unfamiliar bird calls.

"Surprisingly well, actually," I laughed. "Considering I would have been killed the night of the Gala if Aaron had found me first, I'd say I made out ok."

"Once we get into the Silver region, you'll be safe. Aaron can't reach you there. None of the Mystics can."

"Are there really dragons there?" I asked, remembering the Choosing, and the Scarlet's illusions.

Jayce laughed. "You'll have to wait and see, I guess. We're almost there."

I shook my head. "This is all so strange. How is it that you've managed to stay hidden all these years. No one has ever been suspicious?"

"I've had to do things that I'm not proud of, Willow. I had to build up a reputation of a man who shouldn't be questioned, and there's no easy way to do that. You saw how the rest of the Scarlets avoid me. They're afraid of me, and I had to give them a good reason for that." He gazed off into the distance, his mind wandering somewhere that caused his mouth to set in a firm line and his eyes look sad.

I placed a hand on his arm. "Jayce, we all do what we have to in order to survive. There's no shame in it."

"You don't know, Willow. You can't say that when you don't know."

"It doesn't matter to me. Whatever it is, it doesn't matter. Think of all the people you've saved because of it. You're not a bad man, Jayce. Sometimes good people have to do things they regret."

"Willow, I-"

"Ready to go?" Jaxtyn interrupted. Jayce have a quick nod and we started moving south again.

"Lilliana," I asked. "How many Silvers are living in the region right now?" I was curious about my new home.

"A few hundred," she answered.

"Wow, you guys have saved that many?"

"No," Lilliana laughed. "Some of them were already there. A lot of Silvers hid in plain sight, living among other Mystics, but plenty of them had no other choice but to run away. They came here, knowing that it was punishable by death for Mystics to enter this region. It seemed like a safe place to hide. When they got here, they found houses left behind, old and crumbling. They rebuilt, setting up fields and planting crops. The community started to thrive. There's something about the border that keeps them safe."

"What do you mean?"

"I'm not sure. I've actually never been across it. I can't make it over there for some reason. Only Silvers can safely pass."

I turned to look at Eli, realizing what that meant.

"He can't stay with you," Lilliana said softly. "There's a small group of houses just outside the border where visitors can come and stay if they want to see someone living in the region, but they can't make it across the border. It goes both ways, actually. Why do you think the dragons never spread out beyond the Silver region? They can't cross the border, either. They're stuck on the other side."

"How is that even possible?"

Lilliana shrugged, and Xander answered my question.

"Silvers are known to have traveling powers. The best we can figure out, when things were starting to go bad for Silvers back when the war started, the elders got together and created a barrier, allowing Silvers to cross the threshold using those powers, but pushing back on anyone without Silver blood."

"But I don't know how to do that kind of thing! We don't even know yet of traveling is one of my abilities!"

"It doesn't matter! Your blood will let you pass," Xander answered.

"We've been working on trying to figure out how they did it," Jayce joined in. "I'm concerned that the barrier doesn't extend all the way around the region, or that it's weakening over time. I throw Jaxtyn at it sometimes just to see if it still works." He winked at me.

"We are *not* doing that this time," Jaxtyn grumbled behind me.

We all laughed, and I looked towards my brother.

"Don't even think about it, Willow. I won't be part of our weird Silver experiments, " Eli teased.

We walked along in amiable silence after that while I thought about what this all meant. Did I want to leave Eli behind, now that I've found him again? It would be painful to say goodbye to him again. We had the chance to be a family, and once again my blood was getting in the way. Would things every be easy for me?

We camped overnight in a small clearing, eating bread and cheese, and not daring a fire. No use in being so careful getting here just to take such a risk now. We still had a few days to go before I could cross over into the Silver region and be truly safe. We took turns taking watch, but the night was uneventful, and by dawn we had packed up camp and continued our journey south.

When we were just one day away from the border, the

weather turned. Heavy rain fell, making visibility difficult. We squelched through the mud, holding onto each other as best we could so we didn't get lost in the endless rain.

"I don't like it," Jayce said, looking around. "Anyone can ambush us right now. Can you go invisible?"

"I can, but that still leaves the rest of us exposed."

"Getting you there safe is my top priority. You and Xander should go invisible and stay close to each other. If someone attacks, you can run with him. He knows the way."

"And you? Can't you turn invisible, too?" He was a Silver, after all. I hadn't actually seen him use any abilities yet.

"I can, but only for short periods of time. My invisibility isn't as strong as yours. But I can travel. If something happens, just run. I'll get everyone else to safety." He squeezed my hand, and walked back to the front of the group to lead the way.

"If he can travel, then why are we all walking through the mud?" I muttered. Xander had approached me by then, knowing Jayce's plan. He laughed.

"It's not easy to transport other people with you when you travel, especially over long distances. If he did that, he'd have to rest up for at least a week. It's easier to just do it this way unless there's an emergency."

I had so much to learn about Silver abilities. As we walked, invisible, Xander kept up a steady stream of conversation, making me laugh with his goofy stories and easygoing personality. By the time night fell, the rain had let up, though the ground was still muddy. Sleep was uncomfortable at best, but it was worth it. Tomorrow, we'd reach the Silver region. We couldn't light a fire that night even if we wanted to, but at least we had started to dry, and the further south we went, the warmer it got.

I awoke before dawn the next morning, and the rest of the group slowly followed. Jayce didn't force us to leave too quickly, so we leisurely packed up before continuing our journey. We stepped out from the cover of the forest after a few hours of walking, and I got my first glimpse of the Silver region.

The mountains towered in the distance, their peaks kissed with snow despite the warmth on the ground. I could see a river winding through, stretching further than my eyes could see. There were no houses visible yet, but I knew the Silvers were out there, living freely and without fear.

"We should reach the border in a few hours. We'll cut across here now. There are some houses that we can drop the non-Silvers off a few miles southeast," Jayce explained.

"And then what?"

"Then you start your new life, here. Safe and free to be who you are. No more hiding, Willow."

There was a knot in my stomach as I listened to his words. *You*, he had said. *You* will start your new life.

"Jayce, I-"

"I can't stay here with you, Willow. I have to return home. I have a responsibility to the others, the Silvers who are still hidden. I can't turn my back on them."

I nodded. "I understand."

"But," Jayce said, "I can come visit whenever you'd like.

It's simple enough to travel here. I know it well, and I'd just be bringing myself. I can use my abilities, and no one back home would ever know I was missing. Unless, of course, you'd like my brother to come for a visit as well."

I laughed. "Only if you promise I can feed him to the dragons."

"Don't tempt me," he said as he joined in on my laughter.

I turned to look at him, excitement apparent on my face, when his face dropped and he reached for me quickly. I felt a sharp pain on my head, and then everything went black.

EPILOGUE

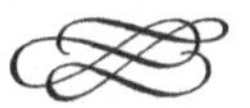

The room turned dark suddenly, although it was still midday. Darker than it should have if there were just some clouds passing overhead. He was here.

The Commoner scrambled to his feet and moved to the corner, cowering with his back against the wall. He knew better than to let them sneak up behind him. He wouldn't be making that mistake again. Even if this *was* a dream, it had real life consequences. The last time they visited him, he had woken up with gash across his face exactly where they had punched him. The outsides of it had been tinged black, and it healed completely within hours. Unnatural.

"You've been talking about me, haven't you, my friend?"

That voice. It was unbearable. Like all his nightmares come to life. There were layers to it, different tones. Sometimes he could swear he heard screams in it.

"N-No, Sir. I would never! Please! I have kept quiet, just as you instructed!"

"Do you know what I do to liars, weakling?"

Two of his minions appear behind him and started advancing forward menacingly. The man backed up tighter against the wall, closing his eyes and praying to the Gods that this was just a regular nightmare. When he opened them, the men were gone, and the stranger sat at his kitchen table.

The stranger laughed, a deep laugh devoid of humor. "You think the Gods will help you, Commoner? They turned their back on you long ago. I'm the only one looking out for you. Come, sit and tell me. You saw her. Did you tell her about me?"

The Commoner approached the table, helpless to deny the stranger's request. He hated being so close. Whoever this man was, he wasn't natural. He was tall. Too tall. His skin was pale like the snow, but his eyes and hair were dark. Darker than anything the Commoner had ever seen. It was more like they were devoid of light than of a specific color.

"I said nothing! I swear it!"

"Good. You know the plan. She mustn't know until it's too late."

The man kept his eyes averted, not daring to look the dark stranger in the eye. He was desperate to wake up, to escape this nightmare. He wanted to see the sunlight. All around him was unrelenting darkness.

"You will be rewarded, Commoner. Remember that. Rewarded beyond your wildest dreams. You're a burden now on them, you know. But if you serve me, you won't be. I can heal you, body and spirit. You can live forever."

"Y-Yes, sir. I will serve you, you know I will!" the man stammered, fear rendering him nearly speechless.

"Good," the stranger said with a satisfied smile. He arose from the table, and again the man was struck by his height, and his unnaturalness. It seemed as if the very darkness moved inside of him, churning shadows creeping underneath his skin, struggling to burst out.

"But," the stranger said, "I was watching you in the woods, fool. I saw you try and warn her. Did you think I could only reach you in your dreams? I am always there, in the shadows. You are never free of me."

Dread filled him, making his whole body shake. "Mercy, sir, please. Have mercy. She is my daughter. My only daughter. I only want her to be safe, and…"

"Safe? She is in a prison, and cannot even see it. What a waste it is, tucking her away behind the borders of the Silver region. But no matter. She will come to me soon enough, and I will set her free."

The nightmare ended abruptly, leaving him panting and drenched in sweat. The sky was tinted pink with the sunrise, and his fear lingered in the air like morning mist.

ACKNOWLEDGMENTS

I cannot express my thanks enough to my parents and brother for their endless support and encouragement.

Also, a big thank you to Gabe for pushing me to keep going even when it got hard, and for always believing in me even if I didn't believe in myself.

I'm also super appreciative for my friends Macy and Haley for standing by my side since day one of my writing career.

And another HUGE thank you to YOU, for giving my story a chance and without you, this passion and dream of mine never would have came true!

ABOUT THE AUTHOR

From the young age of ten, Megan Marie Franey developed a liking for writing and has a natural talent for it. As an emerging author of fantasy romance for young adults, Megan has an affinity for telling great, thrilling stories that captivates the minds of her readers. She started writing as an outlet to escape the stresses of the world and was hooked. Reading books and writing took her to a different realm where she felt at peace and content. Her gripping stories weaved in a smooth flow which makes her writing a solace for many young adults who enjoy her creative storytelling skills. When she is not crafting ideas for her new novels, Megan is a college student who loves to read, write, and travel. She also enjoys spending time with her dog, Ahri.

WANT MORE?

Scan to see my monthly blogs and sneak peeks into my future books!